This is Rebecca Perry's second book. She spends all her spare time reading. She has two sisters, both younger who she is very close with. She lives in Nottingham where she works as a primary school teacher, inspiring her class of Year 4s to pursue the same love of reading that she herself enjoys.

To my grandparents,

Thank you for proof reading this book and I've remembered to number the pages this time.

Rebecca Perry

MY WAR HERO

AUSTIN MACAULEY PUBLISHERS
LONDON • CAMBRIDGE • NEW YORK • SHARJAH

Copyright © Rebecca Perry 2025

The right of Rebecca Perry to be identified as author of this work has been asserted by the author in accordance with sections 77 and 78 of the Copyright, Designs and Patents Act 1988.

All rights reserved. No part of this publication may be reproduced, stored in a retrieval system, or transmitted in any form or by any means, electronic, mechanical, photocopying, recording, or otherwise, without the prior permission of the publishers.

Any person who commits any unauthorised act in relation to this publication may be liable to criminal prosecution and civil claims for damages.

A CIP catalogue record for this title is available from the British Library.

ISBN 9781035899647 (Paperback)
ISBN 9781035899654 (e-pub e-book)

www.austinmacauley.com

First Published 2025
Austin Macauley Publishers Ltd®
1 Canada Square
Canary Wharf
London
E14 5AA

I would like to thank my wonderful family—my mum, my stepdad, my grandparents and my sisters—for being the inspiration behind these characters and future creations.

Monday, 22 November 1943

Miss Daisy Franklin,

We received your reference from Rev J Smith. He writes of your character very warmly, and we would be delighted to welcome you to join our staff at Sutton School starting on Monday, 29 November. Upon arrival, please come to my office and I will give you the tour of the school and let you know the routine for our school day.

You are required to provide your own gas mask.
Yours sincerely,
Mr K Adams.
(Headmaster)

Friday, 26 November 1943

Dearest Mother,

I'm in London. It is simply fabulous here. My accommodations are perfectly lovely and across the hall from me is another girl, Margret, who has been here for a few months already. She was outside having a cigarette and commented on my shoes. I told her that they were my only pair, having given my others to people in my home village. She laughed and said she had done the same thing. It was an instant bond and she offered me one of her cigarettes. We then hauled my luggage upstairs where we discovered that we were to be neighbours.

Margret, or Peggy as she likes to be called, is a nurse at the local hospital. I admire her for that. I don't know how she copes with the blood and death that she must see every day. I think she thinks the same of my job though, being around children all day.

Tomorrow, there is a soldier's dance at the pub. Peggy says that there are always soldiers in need of cheering up. It starts at 4 o'clock and finishes before it gets dark, so that we can all be home and safe in case of bombs and in time for curfew.

I start teaching on Monday, so wish me luck. I've hung my second-best dress up on the wardrobe door so I can get any wrinkles out. I have been asked to do the Christmas nativity, but I am running it with another teacher. The children look forward to this every year, so we felt mean to cancel it. Not when it lights up their faces and brings joy to their hearts. And we all need some Christmas joy right now.

Love to you and father,

Daisy.

---

26 November 1943

Dear Elizabeth,

I've enclosed this letter with the one for Mother as quite frankly, I didn't see the point of sending two separate letters to the same address.

I know we are in the middle of a war, but there is so much activity going on. There are people everywhere and today there was a lovely market on, so I brought two fresh apples.

I'm going to a soldier's dance tomorrow afternoon with my new neighbour, Peggy. We are going to see if there are any dashing young soldiers for us to have some fun with. I'm feeling very grateful for the dancing lessons from the vicar now.

Stay safe, Elizabeth, and look after Mother and Father. Daisy.

Monday, 6 December 1943

Dear Elizabeth,

What a week! I have so much news to share with you that I feel I will run out of paper before I have told it all.

I'll start with my new job. Teaching at the small village school in Kent was great but now, in London, I am in charge of a class of 45 boys and girls all aged between 9 and 11. The children are such an interesting bunch and they welcomed me with open arms. A few of the rascals decided to test me by throwing chalk at my head when my back was turned, but I soon put them right. They won't be attempting that again after sweeping leaves from the school playground.

Feel free to read the first part of this letter to mother and father but I would advise you to keep this next bit to yourself as I feel they might faint upon hearing my news.

I have met someone.

At the soldier's dance on Saturday, Peggy and I walked to the local hall, and upon entering, I simply stood still, taking it all in. The Women's Institute have done the best they can with what little they have, but it still looks absolutely fabulous. There were paper streamers hung from the ceiling and linen tablecloths. Someone had donated a record player and soft, gentle music filled the room.

Peggy pulled me further into the room, introducing me to several women, where we talked for a while.

Then as a slow song came on the record player, a gentleman tapped me on the shoulder and asked me if I wanted to dance. I smiled up at him, taking in his army uniform and handsome face. I accepted and he led me over to the small dance floor where other couples were spinning around or swaying to the music.

This gentleman, this soldier, gently laid his hand on my waist while I rested my hand on his upper arm. His other hand came and took mine in a firm embrace and we started swaying gently to the music. He asked me about myself, and I asked about him. He's been enlisted since 1940 when he and his older brother signed up. He is a medic, so not right on the front lines, which I can thank God for. His brother, Michael, is getting married next week to his childhood sweetheart so they are both back in England for the nuptials. He lost his father in the first war and his mother works in a bakery, but also volunteers with the WI. Apparently, she makes the best jam in London. His mother lives here in London.

I've been rambling on about him, and I realised I haven't even told you his name yet. He is called James Fitz and like I said, a medic in the 35th Division. James is about a head taller than me, so I can tuck my head under his chin like it was made to fit there. He has dark hair, trimmed short but I imagine it would look quite dashing if left to grow slightly longer. His eyes are a deep brown and the way they look at you makes you feel like he is seeing into your soul. And oh Elizabeth, we danced and danced. I don't think either of us noticed when the song changed or even that there was anyone else in the room. I certainly didn't.

When an elderly woman tapped us on the shoulder, we looked up to find that the hall had been emptied and most of the decorations had been cleared up. The woman, whose name was Constance, told us that the hall was closing, and we had to leave. However, she said that she had left us this long because she didn't like interrupting a lovely young couple in love.

I kept my gaze away from James and we both hurried from the hall, thanking the woman. Outside in the evening air, I stood still a moment to let the cold night air brush over me. James asked if he could walk me home and I agreed, not ready for our night to end just yet. I linked my arm through his and we went on our way.

Once at the flat block, I stepped away from James and was just getting my key out when he said that tonight had been one of the best nights since joining the army. I smiled and said I'm glad I could make his evening enjoyable. He then asked if he could take me to the pictures on Thursday which I replied with yes, he could and that he could pick me up from the school.

And then, dear Elizabeth, he leant forward and kissed my cheek, his lips barely grazing my skin. I watched him leave and then went inside. I can still feel my cheek tingling.

How are you and Billy? Is he treating you right? Are you any closer to him popping the question?

I will write soon with news from the pictures on Wednesday.

Yours,

Daisy.

Tuesday 7 December 1943

Dear Daisy,

I shared some of the contents of your last letter with mother and father. They are both pleased that your job is going well, but they are more pleased that you have met a fella. Mother will be sending you her own letter shortly, but I needed to send this before I burst.

Billy finally proposed! I am now an engaged woman who will be getting married in two months, providing Hitler doesn't invade England in that time and my God! I shall be having words if he does! Mother is going to make the dress, so we are all saving our clothing coupons to buy something white. I don't care what the dress is made out of, I would get married in a potato sack. Just so long as I am getting married in St Joseph's, and I am marrying the love of my life.

James Fitz sounds amazing, and you should invite him to the wedding so that I can meet my future brother-in-law.

Peggy also sounds good for you, and I have a feeling that the two of you will be unstoppable together.

Write soon. I'm dying to know about your date to the pictures.

Much love,

Elizabeth.

Wednesday, 8 December 1943

My dear Daisy,

Your father and I are so pleased that you are making friends and have met someone nice. From Elizabeth's letters, he sounds absolutely fabulous, and I can't wait to meet him. It would make us both so happy if you could marry a nice gentleman.

I suppose you have heard from your sister that she is now an engaged woman. William's mother and I were taking bets as to when it would happen and now, she owes me one of her sugar coupons. I shall save it towards a cake for the wedding though.

Your father didn't think we would see the day when William proposed. He was taking so long about it. But young William has come to his senses and is at last marrying our Elizabeth. We hope that you and your soldier will follow shortly.

Love,

Mother.

Thursday, 9 December 1943

Dear Elizabeth,

Firstly, congratulations. Both me and Peggy send our love and wish you the best. I'm going to buy some nice fabric and start making a dress. February will be cold, but the day will be magical, filled with your love for each other.

I received Mother's letter, and can you tell her from me that I have only just met James, so I don't want to scare him off with marriage just yet. As to inviting him to your wedding, we will see; depending on whether he is in the country or whether he sticks around past the pictures. I don't want to call it a date yet in fear of jinxing it. I have started this letter before work and now must dash off before I am late for the headmaster ringing the bell. I really need to find myself a bicycle so that I can get about quicker.

Well, I am home from the pictures, and I am rushing to write all this down before the memory escapes me.

James, Jimmy as he insisted on me calling him, picked me up from the school gate with a small bunch of wildflowers and a smile. He kissed my cheek again and I think that at this rate, I won't be washing just to keep the imprint of his lips on my skin.

We walked on to the pictures and took our seats. I'll be honest, Elizabeth, I couldn't tell you anything about the film as shortly after it started, Jimmy placed his arm round the back of the seat, his hand brushing my shoulder through my coat. After that, the only thing I could concentrate on was Jimmy.

He walked me home because he is a gentleman, and then asked if he could kiss me. I thought he meant on the cheek again, so I said yes. He then proceeded to place his lips over mine, giving me a kiss I won't be forgetting in a hurry. Those sloppy boys back home need some lessons. How did I ever think those boys were good kissers!

Tomorrow, I am getting a bicycle curtesy of Trudy O'Connell, one of the other teachers. She says she never rides hers anymore and after I had mentioned it the other day, she had her husband check it over. He has proclaimed it suitable for use and Trudy is walking it over to school tomorrow. So tomorrow afternoon, I will be riding home from work on my new bicycle.

Looking forward to hearing more news about the wedding plans.

Daisy.

Friday, 10 December 1943

Dear Peggy,

I miss that you aren't across the hall for Horlicks and gossip. I have much news and I have resorted to a letter because I don't think I can keep it inside of me for much longer.

Jimmy came by the school at lunchtime when I was outside, supervising the children on the playground. He waved me over, to a background of children giggling. Peggy, he's asked me out on another date. And yes, I am now counting Thursday as a date, especially after that kiss. We are going for a drive through town as his brother owns a motorcar and Jimmy wants to try it out.

Reply soon or I shall simply fade away.

Your lonely neighbour,
Daisy.

---

10 December 1943

Daisy STOP. Am rushing home to hear all details STOP will be on train tonight. STOP Peggy.

Sunday, 12 December 1943

My dearest mother,

Peggy had the day off today, so we both went to church this morning, and we packed some sandwiches which we took down to the river and ate them, despite the absolute freezing weather. We laughed and spoke of horror stories of the war. Peggy has many more, working in a hospital. In answer to your question, Peggy works as a general nurse. She just goes wherever she is needed most. Yesterday she said, she delivered four babies all before lunchtime from four different women, one of whom was two weeks early.

I am going to ask James to accompany me to Elizabeth's wedding, if his duties permit it. You will be pleased to know that he asked me to go with him to his brother's wedding, but sadly I had to decline due to school. He said he understood, and we have plans to see each other before the wedding.

How is father doing? Is his hip acting up again? He really needs to stop working. No one would blame him.

Much love to both of you,

Daisy.

Thursday, 16 December 1943

Dear James,

I thought I would address this letter to you as James so that we don't appear too intimate with each other. I don't think either of our mothers could cope with the scandal. I also thought it would stand a better chance of finding you this way.

I hope you are enjoying your brother's wedding. I know you asked if I wanted to come with you and I so wanted to say yes, but I couldn't get the time of work at such short notice. However, I would like to make it up to you by inviting you to my sister's wedding in February. I know it is a while away and I don't even know if you will be in the country or not, but if you are, I would love for you to come with me.

The school term finished today. Children are running home to parents, Christmas cheer filling their hearts. This afternoon, we all had a party, letting the children have a free afternoon. The boys ran wild on the playground, the girls made garlands of paper chains and snowflakes, we built snowmen and made snow angels. They were only small though as we only have a couple of inches. I think we will have some heavier snow this weekend which the children are most excited for.

Forever yours,
Daisy.

Friday, 17 December 1943

Dear Daisy,

Nothing would give me greater pleasure than accompanying you to your sister's wedding. I shall speak to my Commanding Officer next week and let you know.

I wish I could have a free afternoon, but I have medics to train. My Commanding Officer told me yesterday that I will be spending Christmas in one of our training facilities so I will be leaving on Christmas Eve. Our first Christmas together and we aren't together. Next year, we will be, I can feel it in my bones and that knowledge keeps me warm at night and sees me through the darkest of days. It is like a light at the end of the tunnel.

All my love,
Jimmy.

Friday, 17 December 1943

Dear Daisy,

Your father is being a stubborn mule. Yes, his hip and both his knees are acting up, but he still insists on going out to work every morning. I keep telling him that there are now two young lads working the fields, both of whom have been trained by your father, but he still thinks he is needed. At this rate, I will have to tie him to the bed to get him to stay home.

It is a shame that you couldn't go with James to his brother's wedding, but I hope he says yes to Elizabeth's.

I read one of your letters to your sister. It wasn't my fault, she had left it open and on the kitchen table and you know me, I am very nosy. I can't believe that young man kissed you in broad daylight. Anybody could have seen you. While I encourage you to spend time with suitors, I don't expect you to be cavorting around London. You have the family name to make proud, you know.

Old Mrs Nelson has been taken into hospital, but is looking perkier every day. She is giving all the hospital staff grief so I think they will let her out sooner rather than later.
Much love,
Mother.

---

17 December 1943

Elizabeth STOP Hide your letters better STOP Jimmy coming to wedding STOP Yours Daisy

---

Saturday, 18 December 1943

Dear Daisy,

I am so sorry. I received your last letter and read it before darting out to meet Billy at the theatre. Mother and father were supposed to be out until later, so I thought I would move it when I got home. Maybe we need to start writing in code from now on.

I thought Jimmy might be coming. I've added him to the list.

I've joined the WI as mother wanted someone to tag along so that she didn't have to sit alone while Mrs Nelson is in the hospital. It's better than I thought it would be, so I am going back next week, although I've made it clear to mother that I will be sitting with ladies my own age.

Are you coming to us for Christmas? Mother says Peggy is welcome to join as well. We don't like to think of you alone in London, especially over Christmas. It won't be a huge affair, but spending time together is what we all need right now.

Keep having fun in London and ignore what mother says about Jimmy. You remember what she was like when I first went out with Billy.

Elizabeth.

Sunday, 19 December 1943

Dear Elizabeth,

Tell Mother that yes, I am coming for Christmas. I will write to her as well. Peggy has been invited to her mother's for Christmas which Peggy is less than thrilled about. However, I pointed out that Christmas is a time for family, but she just scowled at me.

See you at Christmas.

Love,

Daisy.

Tuesday, 21 December 1943

Dear Mother,

I am not 'cavorting' around London with unsuitable boys. I have shared one kiss with one boy – no not a boy, James is a soldier who fights for our country and risks his life for others. Also, he is a gentleman. You really have nothing to worry about. Besides, in a few days, he is going back to his unit, where he will be firmly out of temptation's way.

I think he is the one. He cleared it with his commanding officer and is accompanying me to Elizabeth's wedding.

You also need to stop snooping through other people's letters; one day it is going to land you in more trouble than you bargained for. Give Mrs Nelson a kiss and a hug from me. You could take her a selection of books. It would give her something to do apart from harassing the nurses.

Elizabeth mentioned Christmas in her last letter and my answer is yes, of course I am coming down for Christmas. Could I stay with you over Christmas? I don't mind kipping on the floor or sharing. School term finished last Thursday and Peggy and I are celebrating Christmas together, so I will get the evening train tomorrow.

Do you need me to bring anything? I can make some mince pies.

Also, give father a kiss from me and tell him that he better not be over working himself or he will have me to deal with. Love and kisses to everyone.
Daisy.

Sunday, 26 December 1943

My darling Jimmy,

Merry Christmas! Why you had to leave on Christmas Eve, I shall never understand. I went to Kent for Christmas to celebrate with my family. How I hope that next year, I can bring you to our festive celebrations.

I can't believe that it has only been two days since you went back. A few tears escaped my eyes when your train was out of sight. My father keeps grumbling about the length of the war and saying how if he could get good shot at 'those pesky Germans', then the war would be over a lot quicker. I don't think he is alone. All the soldiers too old or too ill to fight in this war are grumbling. Honestly, father could set up the grumpy old man's club where they can all moan together. I know that's what my mother would prefer.

Although, don't take it to heart. My father is proud of what all the boys are doing, wherever they may be, which includes you, my love. Well, reluctantly includes you after my mother shared with him the contents of a letter to my sister from me, detailing our first kiss. Safe to say, Elizabeth now hides her letters better and we have started writing in code, better than the English Secret Service, just in case.

I keep replaying your parting kiss over in my mind, and I can't believe that I won't see you until Elizabeth's wedding in February. You have my heart with you, wherever you may be.

Please stay safe, my love, and return to me soon.
Forever yours,

Daisy.

Tuesday, 28 December 1943
Dear Daisy,

Christmas went as well as expected. Mother was polite but didn't go further than that. She looked shocked that I still haven't given up work and that look was worth coming down here for Christmas. I would honestly so much rather be at Lavender Cottage with you and your family, but here I am trying not to drink all of mother's 'medicinal' brandy.

I snuck off to give presents to the staff who, as I have mentioned previously, have been more of a family to me than my own. If I had to come home for Christmas, then why couldn't I spend it downstairs with people who won't constantly look down their nose at me?

I am back in London. Work meant that I couldn't spend too much time with my mother – much to my delight. I tried so hard to stop smiling when I told my mother that I would only be staying for two days, but I think the grin still slipped through.

How is Christmas in Kent? How is your sister doing?
Merry Christmas.
Peggy.

Saturday, 1 January 1944

My dearest Jimmy,

This is the first letter of 1944. I woke up before the sun, pinched Elizabeth to wake up and together, we stole out of the house to watch the sunrise over the fields. We brought a blanket and sat huddled together and watched the sunrise over a new day, a new year. Elizabeth and I screwed up our eyes and made a wish, just as we have done for the last twenty years. Granny said it was lucky, but mother always scoffed at that, saying it was nothing but bad gypsy ways. Elizabeth and I like the tradition though, so every year we sneak out and watch the sunrise on the first day of the new year. I won't tell you what I wished for otherwise it won't come true, but I think you can probably guess. Billy joined us, holding Elizabeth's hand and stroking her knuckles with his thumb. I hope to be doing this with you by my side next year.

I can't put into words how much I miss you. Seeing you though the school gate or walking along the river together. My heart pines for you to return, but I know that you are doing something much better than listening to my ramblings about cake and books.

Peggy and I are going to another soldier's dance tomorrow, although I don't want to go if you won't be there. I suppose I have to; I'm playing my part in the war effort after all. Speaking of war effort, Peggy and I have both joined the WI, alongside your mother. She was the one who invited me along and Peggy had the evening off so came with me. We all thoroughly enjoyed ourselves, and I plan to go back next week. Elizabeth was right, the WI is more fun than I thought it would be.

I am knitting you a slim scarf that you can wear under your coat, to hold a piece of me close by you until we see each other again.

Your mother and I are going to meet up next week at the Rose Tearoom to chat further. I hope she has some embarrassing tales of you as a child.

How's life wherever you are? Please keep warm and safe. Thinking of you often.

Forever yours,

Daisy.

Monday, 3 January 1944

Dear Peggy,

I am sorry for how you spent Christmas. Mother would have happily had you. Next year, we shall kidnap you and force you to spend Christmas in Kent.

As you know, I've spent the whole of December knitting various jumpers, socks, and hats. My father always loves wearing our knit wear. Every year, he puts everything on immediately and refuses to take them off for days.

I am glad you wrote to me first, telling me that you are back in London, otherwise I would have sent this letter to your mother, which I don't think she would have been too pleased with.

I'm coming back to London on Thursday, ready for the start of a new school year on Monday.

See you then.

Daisy.

Tuesday, 4 January 1944

My darling Daisy,

Christmas morning dawned clear and bright, the sun shining over a fresh covering of snow. I have all my clothes on and about ten pairs of socks. The only thing that spoiled it was the sound of screaming as men around me cried out in pain from fevers and bullet wounds.

It feels weird to send one letter with both Christmas and New Year greetings, but I couldn't send my Christmas letter so, Happy New Year! With every passing year, I wonder how much longer this war can go on for. I pray, as I do every year, that this year will be the last, but so far God and Hitler aren't listening to my prayers.

Your letters bring me deep joy and make the cold nights seem warmer and the scary, less scary. I keep your letters inside my shirt, close to my heart, because that's where you are. I look forward to receiving your scarf. I shall be using it as a pillow at night, and I shall be smelling it until the scent of you disappears.

Your father has a right to grumble about the Germans, him being a war hero himself. I just wish that my own father was here to grumble at his side.

Our parting kiss plays on my mind over and over. When I next see you, I am planning on kissing you until your knees become weak. That will give you something to write home about. I would much rather be in London with you, listening to all your ramblings. I know you find it hard to believe but I love listening to anything that you say. It sure as hell beats listening to the sound of exploding shells and dying men.

Go to the dance and think of me. I know it cheered me up to dance with a pretty lady, and it sent me back on to the front lines with a smile on my face and a jump in my step. Just don't lavish attention on them like you did me. I don't think I am up to sharing.

I have to be about my rounds. Take care.
All my love.
Jimmy.

Thursday, 6 January 1944

Dear mother and father,

I am back in London. I am scribbling this by candlelight before I go to bed, and I will post this letter tomorrow on my way to the shops. Thank you again for such a wonderful Christmas. Here's to hoping that Jimmy can join us next year.

Father, please go easy this winter. You know that your knees always get worse in January and February.
Stay safe,
Daisy.

Saturday, 8 January 1944

Dear Elizabeth,

Things are looking up. Jimmy and I write to each other whenever we can. I am writing every couple of days and even though he can't write as frequently, he still takes the time to answer my questions, comment on my day and tell me a little of his life in the army.

He is such a lovely person. I can't believe my luck when he asked me to dance all those weeks ago. When I came to London, never in my wildest dreams did I expect to meet someone so kind, so thoughtful and so funny. February can't come around quick enough for us to see each other again, and even that's only for a few days.

Jimmy will be meeting us in Kent, but he is borrowing his brother's motor car, so he will drive us back to London a few days after the wedding. I thought I would show him round the village and let him spend some quality time with Mother and Father.

How is the dress coming along? Mother and Billy's mother, Vera, must be working day and night to have it ready. Do you know where you will move into when you are married? There are plenty of small flats in London, although they are not great for a family.

School is amazing, and the children are all little angels. Yesterday, one gave me a card that said, 'thank you for being the best teacher ever'. I was flattered, but I think I have been her only teacher, so she doesn't have anything to compare it to. But I will take what I can get. Peggy sends her love and give mother and father a hug and a kiss for me.
Much love, your older sister,
Daisy.

Tuesday, 11 January 1944

Dear Daisy,

We are twins, and you are only older by a few minutes!

Wedding plans are coming along very nicely. Vera and mother are working hard on the dress, and we have nearly saved enough sugar and butter coupons to make the cake. It will just be a small one, nothing like the ones we envisioned for ourselves when we were children. But then, none of us could have predicted another war happening.

Billy and I are planning on staying in Maidstone. We have our eye on a lovely cottage across the river. It is called Honeysuckle Cottage and has three bedrooms with a decent sized kitchen. This also means that we are close to Billy's work, and we are both happy with our bikes. The cottage is currently empty and has been since before the war started so we have high hopes. Also, it doesn't need much work done to it, and I can sort most of it in a few days.

I don't know how you cope with small children all day. They would have me running and screaming after an hour alone. It is cute though how much they adore you. The village has taken in so many evacuees and mother has taken two in. They are in your old room, and they are the cutest little things. Both boys, brothers, called Harry and Henry, aged seven and four. They help mother round the house with odd chores, and they like walking down the lane to meet me after I finish work at the shop.

Much love, the better sister,

Elizabeth.

Saturday, 15 January 1944

Dear Mother,

Do you have a plan for the Honeysuckle Cottage Elizabeth and Billy want to buy and move into? If so, I would like to contribute. My earnings aren't huge, but I want to give you a little something towards it. You can tell them that it is part of my wedding present to them both.

I have brought some lovely fabric with mine and Peggy's clothing coupons. I don't have enough for shoes but the ones I have are pretty new, and they go with the fabric I've chosen for the dress. We have whiled away the afternoon gossiping about James and Peggy's new man, Henry.

Yes, you saw that right. Peggy has managed to secure a lovely man who she met a few weeks ago. He keeps coming round and delivering notes for her, or flowers. Or my favourite, sweets, which Peggy shares with me – sometimes. She hasn't told her mother about him yet but all in good time. She said she is waiting for the perfect moment.

The school are treating me kindly, and next week, we are going a field trip to the river, where we shall all take our sandwiches and enjoy the fresh air. The children (and I think the teachers too) need a bit of fresh air and a chance to escape the classroom for a while.

Kiss father for me.

Daisy.

Tuesday, 18 January 1944

Darling Jimmy,

I ran into your mother today while I was in the butcher's. I know we haven't been properly introduced yet, but she is the spitting image of you. Or should I say that you are the spitting image of her. So, I introduced myself and we hit it off right away. She is a remarkable woman, your mother, and I can see where you get your sense of humour from. She had me cracking up right there on the pavement.

I went to the soldier's dance and thought of you the entire time. Peggy taught me a jive though, which I will be delighted to show you in February.

Elizabeth's wedding preparations are going very well. She says that the dress is nearly ready, with just the final fittings and finishing touches to go. I haven't seen what it will look like, but my mother seems to have everything under control and I trust her judgement completely. Her and Elizabeth have also saved enough butter and sugar coupons to make a small cake. I feel cruel mentioning cake, but the vicar said that talking about our lives to you makes you feel more normal and less isolated. So that is what I will do.

My lovely Jimmy, I have laid awake thinking of you these past few nights, wondering if you are safe and well. I would rather have your kisses now to write home about than to wait a moment more. However, I must, and I hold our brief memories close to my heart.

Forever yours,

Daisy.

Tuesday, 18 January 1944

Dear James,

I met your lady friend yesterday at the butchers. Can I just say, why didn't you introduce us sooner? She is a lovely girl whose face lights up when she talks about you, which makes me proud. She told me of how you met each other and that you are planning on going to her sister's wedding with her. I'll forgive you for not telling me you were taking leave and for not spending it with me.

Would you be requiring the family ring? Your brother didn't want it. He preferred to buy his own, and I understand that completely. However, that does now make it available to you. Let me know what you decide.

Stay safe.

Love,

Mother.

Wednesday, 19 January 1944

Dear Elizabeth,

I have so much to tell you. We shall have to have a proper gossip and catch up before your wedding.

But before I burst, I met Jimmy's mother the other week in town. She is lovely, and I know that you will love her just as much as I do. Peggy and I are joining her at the next WI meeting, and I think she is going to teach me how to make the best jam ever. That will be your wedding present, my dear sister, a lovely pot of homemade jam. I am going to surprise you with the flavour.

I'm bringing her to Kent in a few weeks to meet you all.
Much love,
Daisy.

Wednesday, 19 January 1944

Dear Peggy,

While you are living the high life and visiting your mother at Chiswick House, Henry Maddox came round looking for you. He seemed quite smitten with you. I don't know what you said to him to make him get this lost puppy look in his eyes, but he had a bunch of flowers, and a quarter pound of pear drops from the sweet counter. He must have used all of his sugar rations to buy you those! I ran into him in the hall and took both flowers and sweets off his hands for you. I shall put the flowers in water and try not to eat many of the pear drops because I know they are your favourite.

That brings me onto something else. How did Henry know what your favourite sweets are? I thought you had only seen him once or twice. Anyway, I told him you were visiting your mother and that you will be back by the end of the week. He grinned, Peggy, grinned and walked off. I think he was even humming to himself. Congratulations on snagging a wonderfully lovely young man who seems quite nice.

I know that I promised not to eat your pear drops, but I have just eaten one while writing. It is a force of habit, and I didn't even realise I had taken one until it was in my mouth, at which point I didn't think you would want it back. I am going to hide them now behind the cornflakes to try and tempt me not to eat them.

Enjoy the rest of your stay.

Daisy.

Thursday, 20 January 1944

Dear Mother,

I was thinking that I would bring James' mother to see you and father at the weekend. We can get the train down and walk from the station as it isn't far. And besides, she isn't fussy unlike Peggy's mother who I met last week when I came back home from work. Peggy's mother dropped her off at the flat in their motor car. She wasn't driving the motor car, and neither was Peggy, but their chauffer was, who then got out of the car and opened the door for them both. Peggy kindly thanked the man while her mother just ignored him. I knew Peggy was from money and a slightly different background than us, but I didn't realise it was that drastic.

I think both you and father will love Verity, she is such a lovely person to talk to.

See you this weekend,

Love Daisy.

Friday, 21 January 1944

Dear Daisy,

Henry and I might have gone out to the pictures last week where I might have told him about my favourite sweets alongside a few other details about myself. But don't worry, it was a fair exchange. I received lots of juicy bits about him too, which I will share with you only if you promise not to eat my sweets.

I would wait to tell you everything at the end of the week, but my mother has extended my trip. I've told her that I have work and patients that need me, but she thinks all this working nonsense is wrong, especially for 'a girl of my station'. I think I will try and sneak away on Sunday.

So here goes. After meeting Henry at the baker's, we went for a stroll along the high street. I found myself taken in by his charm, so we made plans to meet the following day and then we went to the pictures. He works in a factory, making parts for planes that are shipped over to our boys overseas.

Daisy, I didn't think I could fall for someone like this. He isn't my usual type and what's worse than anything is that my mother will definitely approve of him. And you know that if my mother approves, then there must be something deadly wrong with him. Anyway, I haven't mentioned him at all to my mother. I am waiting for the right time. I think I may be waiting until after the war at this rate. Any sentence that starts with the war, rations, or soldiers she just blanks out as if it doesn't affect her which she thinks it doesn't, her living in a manner and still insisting on having a butler.

Don't you dare eat any more of my pear drops. I will need them after spending time with my mother.

Peggy.

P.S. Can you water my plants? The spare key is under the mat.

Saturday, 22 January 1944

My darling Jimmy,

It still feels odd to write James on the envelope and Jimmy at the top of the letter. I refer to you as Jimmy to Peggy and Elizabeth, but James to my mother. You mother does the same thing, and I think it is a generational thing. My mother still calls Elizabeth's fiancé William instead of Billy.

One of the children at school today said the cutest thing. He came up to me on the playground and tugged my skirt to get my attention. He asked if I was married. I said no, not yet, although there was someone who I had my eye on (that's you, by the way). The child, Thomas, asked if he could be my husband then. He said that if he were my husband, he wouldn't have to do any more schoolwork. I told him that I was flattered, but that wasn't how school worked. Upon finding out that he would still have to do maths and reading, he promptly said that we wouldn't be getting married after all.

Your mother has been sharing all sorts of lovely stories with me about you and your brother, so much so that I feel like I have been there witnessing it myself. My favourite one was by far the story she told me about when Michael convinced you to climb the massive apple tree in your neighbour's garden, which ended up with you getting stuck and then the neighbour pulling his rifle on you. It has provided a lovely image in my mind to mull over as I go to sleep.

Next weekend, I might take your mother down to Kent to meet my parents. She and my mother would get along very well and bold of me to say, but I think it might be worth them meeting each other. I am completely and utterly in love with you, and I can't wait to tell you that to your face.

My family are looking forward to meeting you in February.

Forever yours,

Daisy.

Wednesday, 26 January 1944

Dear Daisy,

Your father and I are planning on giving Elizabeth some funds to help her purchase the house. I believe that William's parents are going to do the same. Thank you for your contribution, your sister will be thrilled. We all had such a good time with James' mother last weekend. When you see her again, please apologise again for me that there wasn't any cake. I am saving all my rations towards your sister's wedding cake.

Have you started making your dress yet? You could always send me the fabric, and I can whizz something up for you. Elizabeth's dress came together quicker than I imagined it would, so I have plenty of time to assist you.

Taking the children out for a nice walk and picnic along the river is a wonderful idea. Just make sure none of them go swimming or you will have soggy children for the rest of the day.

Peggy deserves happiness wherever she can find it, so tell her from me that she should go for it. Although I don't want to hear about any more improper behaviour from either of you.

Are you sure Peggy can't come to the wedding? It would be so nice to meet her. I guess I will just have to settle for meeting her at your wedding to James.

Your father sends his love.

Mother.

Tuesday, 1 February 1944

My beautiful Daisy,

Let me start this letter by apologising for the delay in replying to you. We have been rushed off our feet, with wounded men everywhere, all needing immediate attention. Everywhere I look, there seems to be another open wound in need of my attention or another soldier begging for the sweet mercy of death. I can even see them when I close my eyes.

To help me through it, I am picturing you, dancing the jive, teaching multiplication, and reading, gossiping with Peggy, or sitting writing to Elizabeth. You help me through the bad times.

I am very sorry that you ran into my mother. I was planning on introducing you to each other at Michael's wedding, but circumstances prevented that. Please do take mother to Kent, I think it would be good if they could all meet. I am only sorry that I can't be there with you. Send my love to your parents and Elizabeth. My mother has always called me James and won't budge from it. My father used to call me Jimmy but only out of ear shot of my mother.

I love hearing your chatter, the vicar is right. It does help us to remember that there is a life back home waiting for us. Well for the lucky ones who will make it home. The image of you talking away to a complete stranger made me laugh out loud and I received some very dirty looks from the other doctor. Once I read to them what you wrote, they too were also laughing. I hope you don't mind, but I think we all needed that laugh.

I am looking forward to seeing Elizabeth's wedding dress, though I think my attention may be caught on her beautiful sister.

I will forgive you for almost marrying someone else in my absence, though I am glad you let him down gently. We wouldn't want a trail of broken hearts throughout London. The idea of a child marrying to stop him doing more maths is something that I would have done myself as a child. I bet that's one my mother didn't tell you. And what my mother also failed to mention was that Michael had threatened to burn all of my trousers so I would have to go around half naked. So, it was either the tree or everyone seeing more of me than I wanted them to. Besides, I thought I could easily climb down from the tree once I had climbed up.

I am completely and utterly in love with you as well and if I could I would yell it at the top of my voice.
All my love,
Jimmy.

Thursday, 3 February 1944

Dear Daisy,

Mother told me of the field trip you are taking the children on. It is wonderful for them to get out of the classroom. How many do you have now? You said that you started in November with 45 children. Surely, some if not most of them would have been evacuated by now. I know the village here has doubled its number of children.

Harry and Henry are very cute. They are obviously missing home; I think they are from East London and their home has been caught in the blitz. Harry said their mother is working as a nurse and their father is a pilot. I feel dreadfully sorry for them, and I thank God every day that my Billy wasn't fit enough to sign up. Not that he didn't try several times. I can't imagine what you must be going through with Jimmy. Having the boys here is wonderful, given the current circumstances. It has brought forwards my maternal instincts, and I so can't wait to be married to Billy so that we may start a family of our own.

It was wonderful to meet Jimmy's mother, Verity, at the weekend. I know both mother and father were charmed by her and if her son is anything like her, then he will be a welcome addition to our family – not that you will hear that from mother's lips. She is as stubborn as a mule when it comes to admitting whether or not she likes someone. And I think what you mean by homemade jam is you are going to claim Jimmy's mother's jam as your own, or I'll get a jar of completely inedible goop.

Mother is stressing about your dress. She thinks that you won't have it ready in time or that you have chosen the wrong fabric or wrong colour. It's only because she has finished my dress. She wanted to do something fancy and elaborate, but I stayed her hand and insisted on a simple dress. Honestly, I just want to marry Billy. I don't care what I am wearing. Plus, I feel bad when the whole of England is in waste. Why should I have a fancy dress when others barely have the clothes on their back and no roof over their heads. I have reassured mother that you have been making your own clothes for years now, so you are more than capable of making a simple frock.

I am delighted with Peggy's news about her new fella. Ignore what mother says. I want to hear all about any scandalous details from either you or Peggy. We only live once and especially during this war, we should take every chance of happiness we can get.

I am so looking forward to seeing you next weekend and meeting Jimmy.

Much love to you,

Elizabeth.

Monday, 7 February 1944

Dear Daisy,

Thank you for inviting me to see your family yesterday. They are all simply marvellous people. I have also written to your parents to thank them for their hospitality and the wonderful food your mother prepared.

Meeting your family was such a delight and my only regret is that James couldn't be there to meet them as well. Although I gather that he is attending your sister's wedding with you on Saturday, which will be lovely for you both.

Shall we meet for tea on Wednesday? I can meet you outside the school gates.
Looking forward to seeing you then,
Verity Fitz.

Monday, 7 February 1944

Verity,

Tea sounds wonderful on Wednesday. I have a half day so we could meet at one o'clock.
Daisy.

Thursday, 10 February 1944

Dear Elizabeth,

The field trip proved to be a roaring success. So much so that we will be taking them out of the classroom every other week. They need a chance to run free and just be children, instead of worrying about the war. I know Billy is angry that he couldn't sign up, but he is still doing his part for the war effort. I would rather have Jimmy home with me but then I think we would all prefer our husbands, brothers, and fathers to be home instead of serving armed forces.

Thank you for reassuring mother about my dress. Please tell her that not only is it finished, but it is a respectable length, with gorgeous flowers round the skirt. It is a lovely lilac colour which goes well enough with my only pair of shoes.

Jimmy will come wearing his army uniform, which, don't tell mother, he looks very dashing in. You will look fabulous in anything that you wear, and I reckon mother is secretly pleased that you aren't insisting on a massive gown with a lot of stitching and details.

I can't wait to see you, mother, and father this coming weekend. You must be so pleased that the wedding day has finally approached.

Much love to you and Billy,
Daisy.

Sunday, 13 February 1944

Dear Peggy,

Yesterday was a simply magical day. Elizabeth's dress was perfect, and she looked so graceful walking down the aisle at St Joseph's. Both Hitler and the weather held out and we had clear skies. Clear of rain and bombs. I think Elizabeth is going to put a hold on a honeymoon until after the war. That is, if it ever ends.

But, Peggy, that is by far not my only news. Jimmy came down to Kent the day before the wedding and stayed at The Wellington, our local pub and inn. He promised to kiss me until my knees became weak, and he kept to his word. I think I stopped breathing for a while there and had to be supported by Jimmy's arms for a minute before I could stand on my own. Mother has taken in two evacuees who are in my room, so I was left to share with Elizabeth. I didn't mind; it was like old times when we would creep into each other's rooms at night.

Anyway, Jimmy came down and stayed at the inn. He came over for dinner though and Mother and Father were both instantly in love with him. And you know how much it takes to impress my father. Jimmy and Billy are getting on like a house on fire as well.

The day of the wedding was lovely. Jimmy sat next to me, and we held hands all through the ceremony. We then had a small sit-down meal at The Wellington and dancing followed. Billy made this lovely speech about his love for Elizabeth and how happy he is that she is finally his wife. I had a few tears in my eyes.

And then, as the clapping died down, Jimmy stood up. He said congratulations to the happy couple. And then Peggy, I kid you not, he pivoted, dropped to one knee, and held out this gorgeous ring and ASKED ME TO MARRY HIM! I squealed and said yes. He slipped the ring on my finger and kissed me, in front of everyone there. I know it has been a whirlwind romance, but I have never been so happy in my life. The only dampener on the evening was the knowledge that he is going back overseas in three days.

Please say you will be a bridesmaid. Elizabeth has already taken maid of honour slot.

Many hugs and kisses to you and Henry.

Your newly engaged friend,

Daisy.

Monday, 14 February 1944

Dear Daisy,

I am so happy for you! I jumped for joy when I received your letter; so much so that grumpy Mr Jones came up and told me off. I just stuck my tongue out at him and closed the door. Honestly that man is never happy. I've never seen him with even the smallest smile on his face.

I saw Henry yesterday at the hospital. Before you get your knickers in a twist, he wasn't a patient. He came by to have lunch with me, so we walked to the bakers, brought two cream buns, and walked to Hyde Park, where we found a secluded bench and wiled away, a full half hour before I realised the time and had to run back to the hospital.

My mother is being so stuck up. She keeps writing, demanding that I give up my job and return home. She says she has found a 'suitable man' for me to marry and settle down with. When I first moved to London, I replied to her absurd letters, but now I just crumple them up and throw them on the fire. She doesn't listen to my excuses anymore so there is not much point wasting paper and ink to write them down. She thinks that as a Lady, I should be focused on providing my husband with a warm home and plenty of children. Don't even get me started on the fact that she said, 'someone of my station neither needs nor should be working'. I have reminded her that we are in the middle of a war, but it falls on deaf ears.

Also, my mother has denied soldiers access to Chiswick House as many with halls and land are doing at this time. The hospital is overrun with soldiers rehabilitating, not to mention our regular patients. The right thing for her to do would be to open her doors and let ill and healing people in.

I am working on telling her about Henry, but at the rate I am going, and the way she keeps ignoring every bit of common sense from everyone, it will be my wedding day before she finally realises I am in love.

Yes, I said it. I am in love with Henry, and I don't care who knows it. Well, as long as my mother doesn't find out just yet.

Hurry back, I cannot put into words how much I am missing you.

Peggy.

Friday, 18 February 1944

Dear Daisy,

We have moved into a little cottage across the river called Honeysuckle Cottage. Mother and Father and Billy's parents have given us some old furniture, so we feel right at home. Mother and Father presented me and Billy with the keys after you went off for a romantic stroll with Jimmy. Mother told me what you all did, contributing to buy the house so that me and Billy would have somewhere to call our own. I can't thank you enough, and I will be sure to repay the favour when you and Jimmy tie the knot. After the reception, Billy and I walked to our new home where he lifted me up and carried me over the threshold. Then we just stood there, simply looking into each other's eyes. I cannot believe that I am finally married to the love of my life, that I am finally Mrs William Howard. You know how long I have waited for the privilege of calling myself that. I think I have whispered 'husband' to Billy so many times since the wedding that he may be starting to get sick of me already.

Married life is fabulous, and I love it, and I couldn't recommend it enough! It is the best feeling, knowing that you have married your best friend, your soulmate. We can talk about anything and every night I have a pair of strong arms to hold me close and a comfortable shoulder to rest my head on.

Have you and Jimmy set a date yet? Let me know as soon as you do. Mother has already started saving butter and sugar coupons again.

Much love,

Elizabeth and Billy.

Sunday, 20 February 1944

Dear Elizabeth and Billy,

Contributing to your future happiness is something that I was more than happy to do. I wouldn't want you to be still living with our parents or Billy's family. Can you imagine? There would be no privacy to spend time together as a newly married couple. When Billy carried you over the threshold, I do hope he didn't exert himself too much, we wouldn't want him out of action so that he couldn't work.

Don't worry about saying husband too much. I heard Billy say 'wife' at least five times at the reception when your head was turned. Billy can't be sick of you already, especially not if he has already put up with you for most of our lives. The love that you two share is amazing and everlasting, and I hope that I will share the same connection with Jimmy when we eventually get married.

At school yesterday, I told the children of my engagement, so that when I do get married, they can start calling me Mrs Fitz. I can't wait for that day. The children were delighted with the news and promptly started asking me many questions. I think they did it more to get out of learning their times tables than any actual interest in my life. But it was nice, so I answered their questions as best I could before we went outside for lunch. I resumed mathematics after the lunch break much to the children's disappointment.

Jimmy and I have decided on next month during the Easter break, which I know is soon, but we both wanted to be married as quickly as possible, due to him training the new medics in England.

I will write to mother as well, but please tell her that I will be making my own dress. I have already started it, having been hoping for a proposal for a few weeks now. Peggy thinks I have jinxed it by started before he asked me, but I don't care. Besides, I have had a feeling that Jimmy has been waiting to propose for some time now, so it doesn't count. In my mind, we have been engaged since the first dance we had together.
Much love to you both,
Daisy.

Sunday, 20 February 1944

Dear mother,

James and I have set a date for our wedding. We have decided on next month, during the Easter break and before you say anything, I am not with child, we just want to be married due to James being called away. I want the security of knowing he is my husband, and he wants the knowledge that he has a lovely wife to come home to.

I have started making my dress, so it will be ready in time for the big day, and you have enough on your plate at the moment what with Harry, Henry, and Father.

I heard from Elizabeth the other day and married life agrees with her. I could practically feel the glow coming from the page, as though her happiness has been transferred to the words themselves.

Daisy.

Tuesday, 22 February 1944

Darling Jimmy,

I have told everyone when our wedding will be. I have sent letters to my family, and I met your mother yesterday for a walk in Hyde Park where I told her then. She shed a few tears, out of happiness, I think. She says to tell you that you are a lucky gentleman for snagging someone like me. But I think she is wrong; I am the luckiest person alive to be marrying someone as kind and smart and talented and handsome as you.

I had to reassure my mother that I was not already with child and that our speedy arrangements were simply because we can't wait to be joined in holy matrimony. I was getting ready to deliver the same reassurances to your mother, but she didn't even ask. I assume that this means she knew you were going to propose, and she knew for some time. I'll let you in on a secret, I started making my wedding dress soon after our first dance when we first met. I've wanted to marry you since then, so when you asked me at Elizabeth's wedding, there could have been no other answer but yes.

By the way, please don't apologise for me running into your mother. It is a small town, and we were bound to meet eventually. Wouldn't it have been funny if it wasn't your mother though. Imagine if I just started talking to someone who wasn't even related to you in any way! I wish your father were here too; he and my father would have gotten along like a house on fire.

We still have a little bit of snow in London so the children at school have been outside, throwing snowballs at each other. One rouge missile hit me, which then proceeded to slither down my blouse where it promptly melted. Don't worry, I had my revenge by making the children do a random spelling test.

I am glad that you are not currently abroad but somewhere here in England. Sometimes, I lay awake thinking of you and our brave soldiers (but mainly about you) and how you must be coping. So, when I write to you, I seal the envelope with a kiss and hold the letter to my heart so you may feel me when you open the letter.

Write to me soon, my love.
Forever yours,
Daisy.

Saturday, 26 February 1944

Dear Daisy,

I am sorry for the delay in reply. This week has been so hectic. The boys have become home sick upon hearing the news of the latest bombings. I told them that one of my daughters is living in London, and she would tell me about the state of bombings to reassure them. However, I have told them that their parents are safe and sound, and that they would want the boys to be the best helpers that they can be. Harry and Henry soon stopped their sniffles and asked if we needed help in the garden. I have been giving them plenty of odd jobs to do around the garden and village to help keep their minds off what is happening in London.

Me and your father are so glad that you and young James have set a date for your wedding. I am more than glad to hear that a speedy marriage is not due to pregnancy. Leave that for later dear, there will be plenty of time for that – AFTER MARRIAGE! I remember my own wedding day. Your father was the most handsome man, wearing his officer's uniform, standing, waiting for me at the altar. And that night, well I swear we almost conceived you and your sister right there and then!

I agree with you about Elizabeth glowing. Every time I see her, her eyes are lit up and her smile as wide as the Thames. William also seems happier, lighter almost. Before he proposed, I could sense the weight of the world on his shoulders, but now he definitely seems better, having a lovely wife to help him through his day. Her and young William are settled into Honeysuckle Cottage. They have some scraps of furniture, and I don't doubt that over the years and after the war, they will collect more.

Are you sure that you don't need any help with the dress? I am available if you need me.

Mother.

Monday, 28 February 1944

My darling Daisy,

We have a rest day today. Training new medics is gruelling work but it needs to be done. We need all the help we can get here. Some of the new recruits are barely old enough to shave, let alone face death on a regular basis. But they have all volunteered their service so we train them in battlefield healing; its quick but it gets the job done until we can move them somewhere more stable. So far, we have had three boys fainting, one being sick in the lavatory and one being sick over a patient.

I am glad you have told everyone of our news. I am writing to Michael and his new wife after I finish this one to you. He has been ordered to run the home office here in England, which makes my mother very happy, and it means that he will be available for our wedding. I can't wait for you to meet him. He is a lovely person, who looks forward to our nuptials. He thinks a good party can cure any war related depression.

It makes me so happy to think of you and my mother getting along so well in my absence. Just remember to take everything she tells you with a pinch of salt. Sometimes, she paints me in a worse light and mis-tells what happened. Like when I ran out of a classroom at school, carrying with me all the pencils. I did it because the teacher, who was a rude pig, threatened to throw the board rubber at me if I couldn't recite my tables quick enough. My mother will tell you that I was an annoying child with no respect for my elders.

She is right about one thing though. I am the luckiest guy in the whole of England – no, the world. I am marrying someone who I love and respect and who I can't wait to start a family with. Someone I can't wait to hold in my arms every night.

My mother knew of my intent to marry you, offering me the family ring when you and her first bumped into each other. I think she could tell from that first meeting that we were both in love with each other. Your intuition wasn't wrong, and I can't wait to see you in your dress. Though you will look beautiful in anything you own; but maybe that is just me being biased because I am your loving fiancé.

I am glad I am not abroad, although I would rather be holding you in my arms and dancing away, without a care in the world. I pray every day for your continued safety and that this blasted will end soon so that we can start our lives together.

All my love,

Jimmy.

Thursday, 2 March 1944

Dear Mother,

The boys sound like they are doing okay, under the circumstances. I have enclosed a letter for them both which for one thing reassures them about London. I will let them decide whether they want to share the rest of the contents with you. And you are doing well with them, being their mother away from home.

Don't worry about the time between replies. School is keeping me busy and between that and sewing my dress, I barely have time to see Peggy and write to James.

During the holidays, I am going to pick up sewing to keep me occupied and in money. Our brave boys always need clothes and socks and the like sent abroad, so I am joining the Women's Voluntary Service. Also, Peggy and I have joined the National Fire Service, where for a couple of nights a week, we sit and look out for bombs and the resulting fires, making sure to raise the alarm and get everyone to safety if we can.

I have nearly finished my dress so when it is completed, can I bring it down to Kent? It would be safer with you, outside of London.

Give my love to father and tell him to take it easy.
Daisy.

Thursday, 2 March 1944

Dear Harry and Henry,

My name is Daisy Franklin. You might remember me from my sister's wedding a few weeks ago. In fact, you are both sleeping in my old room. I used to stand on my tip toes to look out of the bedroom window as the sun came up in the mornings. The view is like no other, and I fully recommend it. Even the view from my London flat doesn't beat it.

My mother speaks of you both often to me in her letters and in her last one, mentioned that you are from London. I bet you are missing your parents and your friends. But don't worry, I am sure you will be seeing both soon, just as soon as this awful war is over.

Speaking of London, there is a lot happening here. I don't know where your parents live, but I imagine they are doing what we are all doing, hoping, and praying for the war to end. Me and my neighbour, Peggy, are on fire watch, which means we have to sit about in the dead of night and watch out for any fires that start and put them out as quickly as possible. This week, we have stopped three different fires.

Your parents, wherever they are, would be so proud of all that you are doing to help with the war effort. It is boys like you that make the difference and will bring our soldiers home sooner.

Keep up the excellent work.

Daisy.

Friday, 3 March 1944

Dear Elizabeth,

I am sorry this is such a short letter. We are so busy at school, trying to finish the term on a high note while conducting assessments. The dress is nearly finished and hung up in my wardrobe, at the back with some old cloth covering it to keep it clean. Just a few adjustments and decorations to go.

Today, I saw the first of the spring flowers coming through the cold earth. Their colour is beautiful and vibrant, reminding me of spring times past when we would lay in the meadow together, picking flowers to make into garlands and crowns. Do you remember when we picked those pretty flowers in Farmer Brown's fields, not realising they were actually vegetables? He was so mad, chasing us down the lane, threatening to run us over with the tractor. Oh, how we laughed, hiding in the hedge.

Much love to you and Billy,
Daisy.

Wednesday, 8 March 1944

Darling Jimmy,

It brings me deep joy that you are coming back to London next week. We shall have to go out somewhere, properly celebrate our engagement. Verity wants to go out for tea, and I thought after, we could meet up with Peggy and Henry and go to the pictures.

Tell the boys who are fainting and being sick that there is no place for that on the battlefields, where life and death hang so unbalanced. Although at least they enlisted. It pains me to even think of it but there are people out there who are faking an illness just to stay home. I was going to write 'safe' but what with all the bombing, I don't think anywhere in the world is safe right now.

I think your brother may be right. A good party to take the blues away. Peggy and I recently went out to a dancing club, and I felt a weight lifted off my shoulders. Just having the opportunity to dance our worries away, even just for a few hours, is exhilarating. Obviously, we were back home for curfew but that night, I think I slept a tiny bit easier.

Your mother is a fine woman whose stories I adore. She tells me all about you and Michael as children and the exploits you used to get up to. Is it true that you both hid up in a fruit tree, pelting people with rotten fruit? And is it also true that the old school headmaster caught you and dipped your heads in the pig trough? It paints a very amusing image in my mind, which I cling to when the Germans drop their bombs on us. I hope our own children will be as playful as you and Michael were, although I hope not that mischievous.

My dress is finished, and I am taking it up to Kent this weekend so that my mother can keep it safe for me. Peggy offered to keep it at her flat, but I would rather it be out of London altogether.

I wrote to the two evacuees staying with my parents to reassure them of the state of London. Their parents are still living and working in London and their father is in the Royal Air Force, so they are a little worried. I told them that I thought they were doing a wonderful job of helping my mother around the village. In reply, they have drawn me a picture of them picking potatoes with my father who they call Grump. I can see why; Keith is a hard name to say for a child and Grump suits him better. It is, after all, what he spends his days doing.

Billy and Elizabeth are settling into their cottage wonderfully. They both took a few days off work and spent them together. Now though, Billy has returned back to the factory and Elizabeth has started work with the Women's Auxiliary Air Force. They both look forward to seeing you again.

Forever yours,
Daisy.

Friday, 10 March 1944

Dear Daisy,

Thank you so much for your letter to the boys. They were thrilled. Harry read it out to Henry, who can't read very well yet. I can hear them most mornings, waking up just to see the sunrise. Harry, bless him, lifts Henry up so that they can both see it.

Your words have soothed their hurts in a way I just couldn't. I think hearing from someone in London has made them realise that they are going to be okay, and they have hope for their parents. They write to them every week and so far, we keep getting replies which is good. I don't know what I will do if the replies ever stopped. I pray to God every day for the continued safety of their poor parents.

You worry me sometimes, telling me that you have joined the WVS. But then I didn't raise you or your sister to sit idle while there is work to be done. Elizabeth has joined the local air force division. I thought she would be doing weather reports, but she has proved a quick study in mechanics, so she fixes planes now. We couldn't be prouder of her. At least Peggy is with you so you can keep each other out of trouble, as much as you can. The two of you together reminds me of you and your sister when you were younger, always making mischief.

Your father has been spending everyday with Harry and Henry, either in the garden, planting and picking or walking with them to the shops. I think they are bringing a new flush of life to him, keeping him young. Obviously, he constantly complains about them, saying they are just two more mouths to feed and that they are more trouble than they are worth, but I see the twinkle in his eye, showing his grumbles as a lie. He dotes on those boys, and he will be sadder than I will be when they go back to their own parents. His favourite activity at the moment is to sit in the kitchen, his pipe in his mouth, while he watches the boys write letters to their parents or while they read some of your old books. He always has a smile on his face.

Stay safe and much love.
Mother.

Tuesday, 14 March 1944

Dear Daisy,

Are you glad that the term has ended? Although, having seen mother's letters, I understand that you have joined the National Fire Service and the WVS. Both will keep you plenty busy and will fill your time. I have joined the WAAF, which I didn't think I would enjoy this much. I am part of a team of mechanics, and we all work on planes and their engines. The team is mainly women, with a few men. We all rub along really well, and I have gotten to talking to several of the women about our husbands, our children, and the war.

I have discovered a love for mechanics which is strange because as a child, I was never the one who wanted to get my hands dirty, preferring to leave it all up to you. But now, I cannot imagine wanting to do anything more than throwing on my overalls and getting my hands on a broken engine or plane part. Mother thinks it is scandalous. I am wearing trousers every day to work, which when she sees them, sniffs, and turns her back. As though she will get an infectious disease from them. It makes me laugh every time. I love them though, no flashing your underwear, no trying to stay modest, just freedom. I can see trousers catching on as a fashion trend.

How is Peggy getting on with her job? I imagine she is swamped. I couldn't be a nurse. I nearly fainted when Harry fell over and took a chunk out of his knee. How is she getting along with her fella, Henry?

Billy sends his love.

Elizabeth.

Thursday, 16 March 1944

Dear Elizabeth,

Now that the school term has finished for Easter, I have a little more time to write to you. Have you seen father? According to mother, he is actually smiling and enjoying life. When I saw them this weekend, father was as happy as he was when we were children. Mother is right. Having children around really does brighten him up. You and Billy had better start providing them with grandchildren. They would both make such doting grandparents.

My wedding dress is now hanging up in mother's wardrobe, to keep it away from Harry and Henry. I love them to pieces, but I have worked so hard on this dress, and I don't want their grubby hands on it.

You are right, of course. I can't count all the times you made me wade into a muddy part of the river or pick through the dirt just to get a pretty flower or stone. The image of you gleefully getting your hands dirty brings me deep joy. It is almost pay back for all those times as children when I ruined my dress or got dirt under my fingernails.

Peggy is getting on fabulously. Currently she is working on the maternity ward in the mornings and doing rounds in the afternoon. I sometimes join her for lunch – , quick lunch for both of us. I cycle out to meet her or she will join me near our flats. There have been several days where we have both wanted to just stay there, soaking up the start of the warm weather and forget the war.

I am also doing a little bit of voluntary work for the Red Cross, packaging up parcels for those families who can't get out, or don't have enough money to support themselves. We also package parcels for families who have taken in evacuees. It isn't much but it gives them a little helping hand. Don't tell mother though, what with the WVS and the sewing, not to mention the wedding plans. She will think I am over working myself, but I am not. There are men and women doing far more than I, and I am just happy to play my small part.

I am looking forward to seeing you all next weekend, when I shall be celebrating my love for Jimmy.
Daisy.

Saturday, 18 March 1944

Darling Daisy,

I can't wait for next week. The promise of finally holding you in my arms as my wife keeps me going through the long days and lonely nights. Michael and his wife will join us in Kent on the 26th. It is the only time they can both get away. They will come up in the motor car and bring mother along with them. She said she would be fine getting the train, but Michael insisted. I think that secretly she is happier going in the motor than on the train.

All my love,

Jimmy.

Tuesday, 21 March 1944

Dear Mother,

The plans for the wedding are as follows: I will get the train down on Friday and walk down from the station. I don't need father to come up in the cart. I only have the one piece of luggage. It's not like I own masses of clothes and you already have my dress. Peggy has been kind enough to lend me a pair of her shoes. Her mother refuses to throw any out or give them to people who are in need of them more. They are gorgeous white heels with lace flowers sewn into the sides. Peggy said I could keep them, as she has too many pairs of shoes anyway.

James is joining us on Saturday and his mother and brother are driving down on Sunday morning. They are all

staying at The Wellington. How is everyone? Looking forward to seeing you all at the weekend!
Daisy.

Friday, 24 March 1944

Dear Peggy,

    Hurry up and get down to Kent. My parents are driving me crazy, constantly asking questions about me, you, and London. I need the back up. Stop nursing and come and save me.

    I joke, of course. I will meet you at the station tomorrow morning, and we can walk to my mother's together. Mother decided that you couldn't possibly sleep at The Wellington, so you are staying with us. I hope you don't mind; we can gossip all night. I have reassured her that you are not as stuck up as your mother and would be perfectly happy anywhere, as long as you can get some sleep. I have reminded her that you have patients in worse places than Lavender Cottage.
Hurry up and safe trip.
Daisy.

Tuesday, 28 March 1944

Dear Daisy,

I know I spoke to you before Michael took me back to London, but let me just say thank you again for inviting me to witness such a lovely day.

The wedding was such a fabulous day. James' father would have loved the day. I am glad to see both my sons now settled with good loving women. It makes me rest easy at night knowing they are no longer alone in the world.

Enjoy your honeymoon, and I look forward to seeing you when you are back in London.

Verity.

Friday, 30 April 1944

Dearest Peggy,

Thank you again for being my bridesmaid. The day was wonderful. Jimmy and I have really enjoyed our 'honeymoon' of sorts, staying at The Wellington. We will be returning to London on Monday. We have decided to live in my flat, at least until the end of the war.

Jimmy wants to stay in London, to be close to his mother and brother and I have grown attached to London. My job is there, and I have found some lovely friends (you!) and Kent is only a short train journey away. Jimmy is needed back with his unit so he will be leaving on Wednesday, giving us a few nights in the flat together.

Please, could you continue to keep an eye on my plants. I think the one on the kitchen windowsill is dying, no matter how much I water it. You always seem to have thriving plants, so maybe there is something that I am missing.

The newly named and very happy,
Mrs James Fitz.

Saturday, 1 April 1944

Dear Daisy,

Or should I say Mrs Fitz now? The wedding was magical, and I hope my wedding will be just as magical. I keep hoping Henry will ask but nothing yet. But regardless of that, we are having a wonderful time. A couple of times a week, he meets me for lunch, and we sit on a bench outside the hospital. Sometimes, we venture out further, but after last time, I keep an extra watchful eye on the time, so I am not late. I'll tell you I have never cycled so fast in my whole life when I thought Matron was going to dismiss me if I was even a second late. Henry often comes and walks me home where we share a quick kiss on my doorstep.

My mother is still harping on about me marrying a suitable person. After I turned down the last one, she has just pulled another one out of the barrel. At some point, I am going to have to tell her about Henry, but I am scared that as soon as she knows, she will approve of him and therefore his attractiveness will go away.

Oh, Daisy, what if he doesn't like me because I have lied about myself? He has told me everything about himself, and I haven't told him about my home, my mother – hell I haven't even told him I am actually Lady Margret, not just plain, old Peggy. I love him so much, and I can't begin to imagine what would happen if he were to leave my life now that he is such a big part of it.

I am sorry to burden all of this on you on your honeymoon.

See you Monday,

Peggy.

Sunday, 2 April 1944

Dear Peggy,

Just tell Henry everything. He will understand, and he will still love you for it. Henry seems like the person for you so go for it. And you would have had to introduce him to your mother sooner or later. When you told me who you were, my initial reaction was shock, but I quickly got over that because I know the person under the ladyship. I know the funny, smart, down to earth best friend that I have come to love as another sister. Henry would be mad not to keep you.

You are never a burden; I enjoy hearing your troubles.

See you tomorrow,

Daisy.

Tuesday, 4 April 1944

Dear Mother,

We are back in London, unpacked and ready to start our life together. Jimmy has settled himself into my flat and my life as though he was made to be here. I cannot describe how happy I am at this moment. I have found my soulmate, my other half.

We have decided to stay here, in my flat – well, our flat now. It makes no sense to find another place when James is being called back to his unit so often.

How are Harry and Henry doing after the excitement this weekend? I bet they slept for hours after the reception.
Give our love to Father,
James and Daisy.

Tuesday, 4 April 1944

Dear Elizabeth,

You are right, married life is the best. Jimmy is lovely. We have settled in the flat and Jimmy has made himself at home. The only dampener is that tomorrow he goes back to his unit and won't be back for four months. I haven't written since the wedding as I have been wanting to spend every waking moment with Jimmy. It was a struggle to go on fire duty last night, but in the end, he came with me and kept me company on a building roof.

Peggy has finally told Henry the truth about herself and just as I said, he still loves her. If anything, I think he loves her more. He wants to meet her mother, which just goes to show the strength of his love for Peggy.
Your loving sister,
Daisy.

Sunday, 9 April 1944

My darling Jimmy,

Since your departure, the flat seems bigger and the bed emptier without your presence filling it. To fill the days, I am throwing myself into sewing and the NFS and seeing Peggy for gossiping.

Stay safe, my darling.
Forever yours,
Daisy.

Wednesday, 12 April 1944

Dear Daisy,

I agree with you, my dear. There is not much point finding a new home just yet. Though hopefully this dreaded war will end soon, and we can get back to normal. Well, whatever normal is after the devastation the war has caused.

Mrs Nelson is back from the hospital, but not because she is better – far from it. They needed the bed space so sent home those they could. Me and several others have made a rota to look in on her and give her any help she needs. It takes a village to raise a baby, but it also takes a village to nurse the elderly.

Your father is back to complaining, having taken a break for your wedding. But now, he moans to the boys which they just find funny. He has also started telling his war stories to

them. Harry found two small sticks which him and Henry re-enact your father's battles. He has obviously made himself more of a hero than he was, but the boys love it.
Mother.

Sunday, 16 April 1944

Dear Daisy,

I, well we, have some brilliant news. I am expecting! Found out this morning at the local clinic. I had missed a few monthlies, so Billy suggested I go to the weekly clinic to get a check-up. I went last week and got the test results back today. I am hoping for a boy, but Billy wants a girl. Actually, I just want a healthy baby who has Billy's charm and charisma.

Do you remember what Granny used to say? Hold a ring over your womb and if it swings from north to south then it is a boy and from east to west, it is a girl. Well, we swung my wedding band over my belly, and it just spun in circles. Who knows what that means? Mother says that we shouldn't rely on science fiction when the good nurses at the antenatal clinic know what they are talking about more than her deluded mother-in-law. Personally, I don't mind, as long as he or she is healthy and lovely. Maybe it is too early to tell. You realise that I shall be holding my ring over my stomach every week now until I give birth.

Billy's parents are thrilled. As you know, he is an only child so hopes of grandchildren are resting on him. When I told mother, she screamed and then cried. She gave Harry and Henry a fright as they had just come through the door with a basket of apples in their hands. I think she went straight to her knitting bag to start making a jumper or a blanket for the baby.

Anyway, we are both so thrilled. Billy is over the moon, strutting around like a peacock. We are going to start decorating the nursery, turning the second biggest room into our baby's room.

How are you holding up now that Jimmy is back with his unit? I am counting down the days with you, praying for his safe return.

Much love from a happy mother-to-be,
Elizabeth.

Tuesday, 18 April 1944

Dear Elizabeth,

Maybe its twins! Don't tell Billy that though, he might faint. I seem to remember Granny saying that the ring trick would work from pretty early on. I am holding on to my theory of twins. Granny was a twin and so was father, and let's not forget, us.

I am so thrilled for you and Billy. Mother and father must be so happy, their first grandchild – or grandchildren. I can't wait to be an auntie! I told Peggy, I hope you don't mind. She is very happy for you both as well and she also thinks it may be twins.

I have marked the day of Jimmy's return on the calendar with a big circle round it. For now, I just remember the wedding, and the wedding night. I will also admit to walking round the flat, whispering 'husband' and 'Mrs James Fitz' to myself. It has such a delicious feel to it.

You and Billy will make wonderful parents.

Daisy.

Thursday, 20 April 1944

My darling Jimmy,

Elizabeth and Billy are expecting! She found out last week. Our Granny told us that if you hold a ring over your stomach when you are pregnant, you can tell if the baby is going to be a boy or a girl, depending on which way it swings. Anyway, she swung her ring over her belly, and it just went round in circles. Mother thinks it is a load of superstitious nonsense, but I think it is twins. Are you on the twins or single baby side?

Peggy found a copy of *The Little Prince* which I am now halfway through. It is a simply wonderful book. It is a tale of a boy from another planet and his galactic travels. I haven't been able to put it down and was nearly late for work yesterday. I had to pedal faster than I've ever pedalled before. Don't worry, I made it with one minute to spare. I'll keep hold of it for you to read when you are next home. Ahh, home. With me. What a statement that is. I can't wait for you to come home, me being held in your arms as we dance together.

Father is being grumpy again. I think it is the changing season, though spring is his favourite season. Harry and

Henry are keeping him entertained though, all three of them battling it out in the garden with sticks and bin lids.
Forever yours,
Daisy.

Sunday, 23 April 1944

My beautiful wife,

I just like saying wife – a lot. I have been telling all the soldiers I am treating. I think my commanding officer would like to shoot me just for the goofy grin permanently on my face. But I can't help it, I am happier than I have ever been, even though I am currently wading through mud and treating wounds with dirty bandages and no clean water.

I am delighted for Elizabeth and Billy. Tell them that I think your mother is right. Sorry, but as a medic, I can't see the logic in a ring determining the sex of the baby. Twins though, it could be. You, yourself are one part of a twin so I assume it runs in your family. I think I would quite like twins. Two little girls, with their mother's smile.

I'll let you in on a secret, I started reading *The Little Prince,* but I couldn't get past page ten. I am more of a George Orwell fan. But I imagine, hearing you read out loud, your head in my lap as I stroke your hair, listening to your lovely voice, may change my opinion of the book.

I think your father has become a young man again, seeing two young boys running round his house. You will have to keep an eye on him to make sure he doesn't get a second wind and enlist. Home for me is wherever you are, my love, in your arms.

All my love,

Jimmy.

Wednesday, 26 April 1944

Dear Daisy,

I can't picture twins. How would I manage? Mother always seemed stressed with us. Although can you blame her? We were probably the worst children in the village. You always getting muddy and ruining your clothes and me terrorising the local farm animals. Can you imagine if I had children like we were? Mother would obviously find it hysterical.

Billy read your last letter over my shoulder but to his merit, he didn't faint. He thinks twins would be great. I don't mind you telling Peggy. I want to shout it from the rooftops so you can go spreading it round the whole of London and I won't bat an eye. I think I have already told everyone in the village at least twice now. Besides, I consider her one of us now, part of the family. Who wouldn't, with a boorish hellhound for a mother. Peggy really needs to step up and tell her mother about Henry. He seems like such a lovely person.

Jimmy will be back before you can blink.

Much love,

Elizabeth.

Sunday, 29 April 1944

Dear Elizabeth,

I have news. Peggy is married! She left yesterday to go to the pictures with Henry and came back a married woman. She apparently got fed up waiting for him to propose so she asked him. She said 'will you marry me? Today?' He said yes. So off they went and are now married. I am only cross that she didn't tell me beforehand. But I am sure that her mother will insist upon a grand wedding at Chiswick House. I suspect that Henry was already thinking of marriage, but Peggy has always been a little impatient.

School starts back up on Monday, and I cannot tell you how excited I am to be going back to work to see the children. I know at least ten of them have already been evacuated to the country, but I think more will have left over Easter.

We weren't the worst children in the village. Those Smith boys were horrible, always throwing mud and sticks at us. If you had twins like us, you would love it. And I know Billy would too.

Much love to you all,
Daisy.

Thursday, 4 May 1944

Darling Jimmy,

School has started back up, and I am so glad to be back in the classroom with the children. One of them has drawn me the loveliest picture of their parents outside their home. The child's father is in officer's stripes, so I wonder where he is serving.

I told the children of our marriage, something to cheer them up after the bombing over April. They all cheered. I think they would like you. I then spent the morning answering questions about you and our wedding. One child started crying though and when I asked why, she said she wanted to be invited to the wedding. So, I've told her, and the rest of my class, that when you, Jimmy, are back in London, you are coming into school and we are going to have a party, of sorts. You don't mind, do you? It would make the children so happy.

London is empty without you, so hurry back to me.
Forever yours,
Daisy.

Sunday, 7 May 1944

Dear Mother,

First week back to school went well. My class is now down to 20 from 45. Honestly, I am surprised we still have this many left. Some of the children are worried about their classmates, so we spent the afternoon writing letters to them, telling them of life in London and asking how life is in the country. I think it helped and I am going to the headmaster's office on Monday morning to demand that they be sent on. I'll even pay for the stamps, and I feel the children deserve and need to be in contact with their friends.

I've slowed my schedule with the Fire Department, but I need something to keep my mind from dwelling in some far-flung corner of England and of course James, in the evenings. What did you do when father was fighting in the first war? How are Harry and Henry?

How are you and father doing?
Missing you all lots,
Daisy.

Wednesday, 10 May 1944

Dear Daisy,

I love Billy, and I love that we are starting a family, but what I do not love is the nausea. Every morning it seems, I can't even keep down tea and toast. Billy keeps saying I should stop working but I seem to feel better after emptying the contents of my stomach. Besides, I am not even showing yet. And what would I do with myself all day at home while Billy is working? I've told him that I shall be going to work until I can no longer see the parts in front of me. I will ask the nurse when she calls in on her rounds, just to ease my (and Billy's) mind. Mother says it is normal and when she was pregnant with us, she was constantly being sick. Drove father mad apparently.

I am glad for Peggy. She deserves every happiness that you and I now have. I bet her mother wasn't too pleased with the sudden decision. She seems like the type of woman who would have insisted on a massive wedding, regardless of the war going on around us. She probably considers the war a huge inconvenience.

If she does throw a big wedding though, try and get an invitation for me and Billy – baby permitting. I would love a good party, and I think Peggy would like all the support she can get.

I have a mental image of you sitting by the door, clawing, and whining to be let back into the classroom. Much like our old dog when we were ten.

Give my love and congratulations to Peggy,
Elizabeth and Billy.

Saturday, 13 May 1944

My darling Jimmy,

I came home from school and went to the shops with Peggy and Henry, Peggy's new husband. They married last week, in secret, much to her mother's disgust. Peggy is happy though and that is all that matters.

I had some new students in my class today. Three boys and two girls who have all just turned nine so have been brought up to my class. They were supposed to come up at after Christmas but there were a few issues with their records.

I sat down to write this letter to you but only got as far as the first line due to bombings. Had to run down to the shelter. I took my pencil and paper though so I can continue to write. So, this letter is currently being written in an Anderson shelter down the road from our home. Last time I was in here, we weren't allowed out for hours. Someone had brought a book though and started reading it out loud to keep the small children from getting too restless. I found myself listening in and groaning alongside children and adults alike when we were given the all-clear. I might have to see if the woman is here now so that we can either finish the story or if I can borrow it. The suspense has been eating me alive. I HAVE to know what happens!

I bet you are laughing to yourself about my reading obsession. Just tell your fellow soldiers that your wife is a bit mental. The children at school have already said as much about me, based on my wacky lessons.

Speaking of the children, they keep asking when you are coming to our party. I have reassured them that although you desperately want to come here for a party, you are doing very important work that I can't pull you away from. One has drawn a picture of me and you. Well, what they think you look like. I don't think you have a three-foot long neck and giant feet. I could be wrong; you could have hidden them from me so that I would still marry you.

I saw Verity yesterday; we had tea and then went for a stroll together. I called her 'Mrs Fitz' as I have always done but she insisted on Verity. It feels a bit weird coming of my tongue, but she reckons it will soon come naturally.

Your loving wife,

Daisy.

Wednesday, 17 May 1944

Darling Daisy,

I hasten to assure you that my neck is quite normal as are my feet. In fact, I have a doctor's form and signature that proves I am healthy, whole and everything in working order. I must confess to having one little toe slightly longer than the other, but I promise to forever keep my socks on.

A party with your delightful children would be lovely. I can't say for definite when I will be back as things are still as bleak as ever here. But you can tell them that the next time I am in London, the first thing I will do is hold my wife in my arms, kissing her until she can't breathe and the second thing I shall do, is come to 'our wedding party'. Actually, maybe just keep the first one to yourself, the children don't need to know that just yet.

I thought Henry was proposing to Peggy? He and I spoke at our wedding, and I know that he had plans to ask her, I just didn't know when he was planning on popping the question. Good for them though. I know the feeling of wanting to marry the woman I love, just so that I can hold her close every evening and kiss her awake every morning.

I am sorry about the latest round of bombs. Was anyone hurt? Any buildings down? What book and was it Mrs T from two floors down? Whenever I see her, she always has a book tucked under her arm or in her bicycle basket. It is such a lovely sight that even in the midst of a war, she is still finding time to read, still being able to find a little bit of happiness.

I did indeed laugh out loud, earning myself a look from a fellow doctor. I explained that my wife loves reading and was disappointed when the Germans stopped bombing London as it meant that she couldn't finish listening to the book someone was reading out loud. But it then led to a conversation about both our wives and how much we miss them. It passed some time and managed to take our minds of the tragedies that we face every day.

My mother loves you and if she didn't, you wouldn't even be able to call her 'Mrs Fitz'. It would be 'Madam'. She wrote to me a few weeks ago, saying how much she loves spending time with you. I know that she feels my absence almost as much as you do, so the time you spend with her is precious.

I like hearing you say our home, it makes me sleep at night when it is otherwise impossible. Just the knowledge that when I next come home, I won't have to stay with my mother or Michael. That I can come home to you and our home.
All my love,
Jimmy.

Friday, 19 May 1944

Dear Daisy,

I must apologise for the late reply. The farm has been hectic these last two weeks. Your father and I have been working overtime with Patrick, the farmer. We haven't been hit at all, which I am forever grateful for, but we all like to be prepared. Can't have those infernal Germans bombing our fields, can we? Harry and Henry have been doing their part, alongside most of the children in the village. Londoners and villagers alike are joining forces to help the community. It is a lovely sight, but then I remember that we are only joining together like this due to the war.

I wish you wouldn't stay with the National Fire Service. I don't like the thought of you up on rooftops with naught but

Peggy and a flashlight for company. But at least you are doing something towards the cause, no matter how dangerous. I understand the need to fill your time though. I was the same when your father was away fighting. The days were fine as I worked, using every second of daylight I could get to occupy my fingers as well as my mind. The nights were the hardest. I couldn't sleep; a reel of scenarios going through my head, everything from your father coming back home to me to the worst possible outcomes. We had decided to wait until after the war to start our family, which sometimes I regret. If I had a baby to concentrate on, I might not have been so lonely. That is why I am so glad that Elizabeth is expecting, and it is my hope that you too, will soon start your own family with young James.

On to happier topics, Elizabeth told me about Peggy marrying her young man. Even if the actual event is a bit fast and sudden, I am glad she has found someone. Has she told her mother yet? I still can't believe that she asked him! What is this world coming to?

The boys are wonderful, keeping busy by helping out with the garden. They are now attending the village school which they both love. I think they like playing with the other children but not the schoolwork though.

How is London? I managed to get a copy of last week's paper, and before it was put on the firewood pile, I read about the recent bombings. There have been several quite close to you and Peggy, so I hope you are both keeping safe. I care a lot about the both of you but please spare me the details, I wouldn't be able to sleep at night.

Your father is fine. He is currently having a nap before dinner. Working the fields makes him more tired than he wants to admit.

Mother.

Monday, 22 May 1944

Dear Elizabeth and Billy,

Peggy suggests ginger biscuits. I managed to find some, so I have enclosed them for you. Feel free to hit Billy if he attempts to eat one. Last I saw, he isn't carrying twins! I think you should keep working but go easy. I don't want you or my nieces or nephews to fall ill because of your working.

Billy, please keep an eye on my troublesome sister. She doesn't know when to stop and rest. When we were twelve, she had the measles but thought she was well enough to go to school. So, she crept out of the cottage when mother wasn't looking and ran down the lane to school. She ended up giving US ALL the measles and school was closed for a month. I know that nausea is common in pregnant ladies, but I do worry over her. Just please, make sure she isn't overworking herself.

I was much like our old dog, sitting and scratching the door. What was his name? Father doted upon him; do you remember? But yes, I was annoying Peggy and the rest of my neighbours so much in the first week or so, I was advised to find something else to do with my time. And that's how I found the VFS and mending clothes, first for people in the building and then for others down the street.

I think Peggy's mother is planning something extravagant. If you don't get an invitation, Peggy has already agreed to sneak the both of you in.

London was bombed again last week and I, alongside the rest of my neighbours, had to go down to the nearest shelter and wait it out. I took the letter I was writing to Jimmy though and this one was quicker than the last. Please don't tell mother the bombs were so close. She knows there was a bombing, having managed to get hold of a London paper but she doesn't want the details. I don't want to give them to her either as I know she worries about me living in London. Could you reassure her that I am doing okay, and that I am taking every precaution I can?

Much love,

Daisy.

Wednesday, 24 May 1944

Dear Daisy,

HELP ME! Henry and I took the mail train over to see my mother to tell her of our marriage. The journey was lovely if not a bit bumpy. We then walked arm in arm from the station to my mother's house. The day was surprisingly warm and halfway there, I had to stop and remove my coat. It is really lovely when the spring weather is here to stay.

Anyway, I wanted to distract myself and you from the horrors of yesterday, but I just ended daydreaming, reliving that wonderful time when it was just the two of us and my mother didn't know.

So, we knocked on the door and Jeffery opened it. I hugged him and introduced Henry. Jeffery has always been so much more than a butler to me. He was the one who actually spent time with me as a child, and he taught me how to get a good reach when throwing stones. And who still even has butlers nowadays? I feel like saying 'It is the 1940s, Mother, even people in London don't have servants anymore'.

Hearing the commotion from the day room (I kid you not!), my mother walked out. She stopped in her tracks upon seeing me, and I think her jaw hit the floor when she saw Henry. That caused me to very nearly laugh out loud.

She sweeps forward, and says 'thank you, Peters. That will be all. And who is this then?' all in one breath. She has never treated anyone who works for her as anything more than glorified furniture. 'Mother', I said, 'this is my husband, Henry Maddox. Henry, this is my mother, Catherine.'

And what was her response? No sweeping hugs or handshakes. No kisses on the cheek. Not even a 'welcome to the family'. No, her response to Henry was 'Lady Catherine, to you' and then to me 'Are you with child then?'

Can you believe that? I thought she would be happy that I had found someone as lovely as Henry. I thought she would at least respond with politeness her upbringing had drummed into her. I was mortified. I very nearly walked out there and then, and it was only Henry squeezing my fingers that calmed me down enough to answer my mother and stay in the house.

I also can't believe that she thinks I am pregnant! That no one would have me unless they had knocked me up first!

Henry then proved what an absolute angel he is by answering my mother, telling her how we met and how and when we were married. I think I have fallen a little bit more in love with him when he stood up to my mother for me. Anyone who can do that and remain standing deserves a medal.

The fact that I am writing this letter to tell you about it all and not sitting on your sofa is testament again to Henry's love for me and his wish to see us do the right thing.

Once my mother had gone back into the day room, I turned to Henry, asking to go. He just kissed me, his love flowing through his lips and into me, giving me the courage I needed to follow my mother.

He really is a wonderful man, who I do not deserve, and I will love until my dying days. I just hope that if we do start a family of our own, I won't turn into my mother.

I am sorry for the rant, but I couldn't wait to tell you. I was positively bubbling over with rage and anger, all directed at my mother. I confess to throwing a vase through the still open front door, but it was a truly awful piece that didn't even have any flowers in it.

We shall be returning to London by Saturday at the latest, even if I have to climb out of my bedroom window like I did when I first escaped to London. Pray for me. I will need all the strength I can get, spending three whole days with my mother.

Peggy.

Thursday, 25 May 1944

Dear Peggy and Henry,

I addressed the envelope to just you Margret, but the letter is for both of you. No sense enraging your mother further. I am writing this during break while eating my lunch, so excuse any crumbs.

The weather is so nice here, so hurry back so that we can sun our legs together. We have been extending the children's time outside, letting them play for longer. There are times when they aren't allowed outside due to the bombings and such so, we like to see the children outside as much as possible.

I hope you don't mind but I copied out your letter to both Elizabeth and Jimmy. Both could do with having a laugh and I know that your mother's antics will provide that humour. I've given strict instructions to Elizabeth not to share it with my mother or we will have a riot on our hands.

I suppose that there are quite a few windows and plant pots with holes in them. Let me guess, stone throwing was a secret lesson that your mother certainly wouldn't have approved of.

I actually fell over laughing when I read 'the day room'. Do you really have one? Do you also take tea in the drawing room and eat your evening meal round a big twelve-seater table? It is a massive leap away from eating chips straight out of their newspaper wrapping on our laps. Do not worry, I will not be treating you any different when you return home, as I am sure Henry won't either.

I can't believe she pulled the 'Lady' card. Who even refers to their title anymore? I thought that had died out fifteen years ago!

You and Henry are perfect for each other and don't let your mother persuade you otherwise. Given time, she will see the love you both have for each other and that you belong together. I think she is just upset that you got married without telling her. I understand your reasons behind it would encourage you to do so again if we could go back and do it all over again. Just try and be patient with her. And if that doesn't work, you'll be in London soon enough.

Peggy, you definitely will not turn into your mother. You are too kind and loving and caring to do that. Besides, if I sense you turning into her, then I'll slap you. Henry will also be a very calming influence on you, so between the two of us, you will be a wonderful mother.

I'll look out for you on Saturday, send a telegram when you have left your mother's. Please don't climb out of the window, you have a third-floor room, and it gives me the shivers just thinking about it.

Your loving friend,

Daisy.

Sunday, 28 May 1944

Dear Daisy,

Ginger biscuits worked. I wrinkled my nose at them first, I didn't see the accompanying letter, so I thought you cruel for sending me biscuits I don't like. But once I got past the taste, I ate two and haven't been nauseous for a whole day. So, thank you. Billy has just rolled his eyes, seeing how long it took me to write that.

Thank you also for a copy of Peggy's letter. I do hope she doesn't mind. I shared it with Billy and we both had tears running down our faces. I must say though, well done Henry, for standing up to 'Lady Catherine' like that. It would have made me run screaming, that's for sure. It makes me thankful for both mine and Billy's families and that everyone is so loving and supportive. At least Peggy has you and now Henry.

I cannot believe that you are still on the twin's train! Everyone has come to the conclusion that it is just ONE BABY. Although if you are right after all of this, I think I may have to hit you.

I did not give measles to the whole school, only most of the children actually came down with the spots. They only closed the school because it wasn't worth opening for only five children. Both of us are taking yours and mother's advice though and I am taking it easier. Still working, just not doing as much heavy lifting.

The dog was called Patch. Father used to grumble and moan about him and would refuse to take him for walks and then one day, we came home from school to find Patch and father sitting together in the garden. They were best friends from that day onwards, even though father used to deny it with every breath. Come to think of it, father was the same when Harry and Henry first came to live with us. But now, to look at them, you would think that father has had two more children, the amount he dotes on them.

Don't worry, I understand your thoughts behind not telling mother. She would only insist you come back to Kent, and I think there is nothing more for you here. You are a fabulous teacher who needs to be in a school with a bigger student population than twenty in the whole school. As much as I would love for you to come back and live here, I know you are happier in London.

Work is going wonderfully. I feel that I am helping the war effort and not just sitting at home, waiting for my husband. It looks like both of us have found what we were born to do.

Much love,

Elizabeth.

Monday, 29 May 1944

Dear Mother,

Don't worry about the time in between letters. I am glad you are keeping busy. School is going very well, the children loving the good weather and the opportunities to spend more time outside.

You know that the Germans aren't targeting smaller villages, only bigger cities, places of importance and usefulness. Thankfully, my flat is still standing, despite some nearby bombs. I am taking every precaution I can, making sure to keep to curfew and get to the shelters as soon as the sirens go off.

I didn't realise you were so lonely without father. Hearing of your struggles and how you coped with it all, has made me thankful that James is a medic and not a soldier fighting death at every turn. Of course he is, but he himself isn't at risk of being shot.

Peggy has told her mother about the marriage. Her and Henry went down together and told her. Henry stood firm beside her the whole time, and I think Peggy's mother is close to accepting it. She and Henry are now back in London, both their work schedules making it necessary for them to be back in the city.

Harry and Henry will both be in Jane's class then. Please warn her about them. She was always so sweet and kind during our time working together. I don't think she could handle the antics of two London boys. Give father a kiss for me.

Love,

Daisy.

Friday, 2 June 1944

My darling Jimmy,

Did you get Peggy's letter? Well, my letter, in which I copied out Peggy's words. Imagine if our own courtship and marriage was like that. I think I would have done as Peggy has done and asked you myself. You are lucky that you proposed when you did, otherwise I think I would have hauled you in front of a priest before you could blink.

I am glad to hear of your doctor-approved healthy body. The children were disappointed though that you weren't seven feet tall with giant shoes. I didn't tell them of the longer toe. They would think you a monster. Recalling your feet, I don't think one toe is longer than the other. But then again, I wasn't paying much attention to your feet when we were together.

I definitely will not be telling them about any desires to hold and kiss your wife. I don't think I could ever utter the words aloud unless they were to you. I can't believe you didn't tell me Henry was planning on proposing to Peggy. I would have kept it a secret and when someone says, 'don't tell anyone', everybody knows that your wife doesn't count! I will forgive you though, as they are now man and wife, forever more, and will hopefully start a family soon. I am hoping to be in line for role of godmother.

It was Mrs T! It was *Through the Looking Glass,* a sequel to *Alice in Wonderland.* So, I've managed to borrow it and I finally read the ending. It was wonderful. I ran into Mrs T yesterday and we got to talking about the book. She suggested I read it to the children at school at which I heartily agreed. So, I rode to school this morning, the book tucked into my basket. I am saving it for an afternoon treat, otherwise we will never do any literacy or mathematics.

I miss you more than I can express into words. Hurry home soon, my love. I will kiss the seal of the envelope for you.

Forever yours,

Daisy.

Sunday, 4 June 1944

Dear Elizabeth,

Of course, the ginger biscuits worked! Do you really think I would give you bad advice! I don't go giving out bad advice. Ignoring the time, I told the neighbour's son he should be a tight-rope walker before he proceeded to fall of the rope and into the river. It was a good thing he could swim!

What I wouldn't have given to be a fly on the wall when Peggy told her mother she was married! Honestly though, her heart must have been hammering in her chest. I know I was nervous for Jimmy when he stood up and asked to marry me at your wedding. It makes me very grateful not to be a man. Having the pressure to stand up before the person you love and propose. And what if the lady rejects the proposal! It just makes it doubly bad.

I will not mention the twins again, but I am making two christening gowns, just in case. And I will hold on to my 'I told you so'. If, by the longest shot and some great fluke, I am wrong, I can always keep the second gown for my own baby. Before you start protesting though, I have cut up my old sheets, having washed them thoroughly first.

I remember Patch now! He was such a lovely dog. I cannot believe that father didn't want the dog in the first place and then became the most attached to it. Do you remember when Patch stayed out one night and father was frantic, insisting on going out and getting a search party together to look for him? School is going wonderfully. The children, though we are now half in number, are all lovely.

Take care of my niece/nephew and Billy.

Love,
Daisy.

Friday, 9 June 1944

Dear Daisy,

Before I could warn lovely Jane about the boys, I was called in to speak to her in the classroom. Honestly, it is like I am reliving my nightmares from when you and your sister were terrorising the teachers. Some days, your father walks up the lane to the school to pick the boys up and sometimes I go. The boys obviously prefer your father as he lets them run through the fields and the mud, picking up sticks and rocks to fill their pockets with. I am slightly stricter, making them stick to the paths.

When I got to the school yesterday afternoon, Jane was standing at the door, seeing children to their parents and evacuees to their guardians and she noticed me and beckoned me towards her. My mind went to the worst possible places, and I was all ready to start apologising profusely. However, the issue was that after having a piece of chalk thrown at Harry, he threw it back. I had to stifle a laugh behind my hand. Of all the things that they could have done and believe me, Elizabeth has been telling them what the two of you used to get up to, it was only throwing a piece of chalk!

Walking back to the house, I asked Harry about it, and he said that it wasn't fair. If teachers could throw chalk for a slightly slow answer, then he should be allowed to throw it back. Once again, I stifled a laugh, but I didn't try as hard as before. Harry also said that he only hit Jane on the shoulder, even though he was aiming for her head.

I've enclosed some lace I found at the market which will make a lovely trim on that christening gown you are making. It will make a perfect finishing touch to what will be a beautiful piece of clothing.

Please make sure you are staying safe. I still think you should come back to Kent, but I know you love Peggy and the school and London. Your father says hello and passes on a kiss and a hug.

Love always,

Mother.

Tuesday, 13 June 1944

Darling Jimmy,

Something delightful happened this week. When I was at the bakers, I found a copy of *Murder on the Orient Express*! Just lying on the floor, abandoned. I had a copy as a girl, but it was destroyed when I leant it to the neighbour's boy who promptly threw it down the disused well. I managed to fish it out with the help of Elizabeth, a bucket and several pieces of rope knotted together. When I pulled it out of the well, the book was wet though, and covered in a mixture of slime, rotten leaves, and broken twigs. It was a shame, both me and Elizabeth loved that book, and we would often read it out loud to each other.

So, when I found the book again in the bakers, I was amazed. Mother had refused to buy us another copy, claiming that she thought it was us who threw the book in the well in the first place (we had done something similar to one of her gardening books before). I asked everyone in the shop if it belonged to any of them or if they had seen who had dropped it. Everyone, including the baker and his apprentice, didn't know. I asked if I could keep it then and no one had any objections. So now I have a slightly battered but loved copy of one of my favourite childhood books. I shall take it into school so that the children can enjoy it as well – though obviously not before I have read it myself. I am halfway through already and had to tear myself away to write this letter to you so I could get it to the post office in time.

I am gazing longingly at it though.

Apart from the miraculous finding of *Murder on the Orient Express*, life is dull without you. I pray for your safe return every day, hoping to find you on my doorstep when I get back from school.

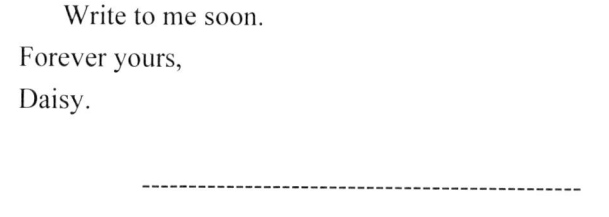

Write to me soon.
Forever yours,
Daisy.

Thursday, 15 June 1944

Dear Daisy,

Harry and Henry came round yesterday. We had a cup of hot milk together. Harry told me what he did to poor Jane, and I nearly fell out of my chair. I was laughing so hard! I suspect mother wasn't so pleased, but Harry is now looking very smug. Honestly, when the war is over and we return them to London, their parents are not going to be as pleased by us, teaching their boys 'naughty country ways'. I may consider changing my hair and name.

Your advice, while often amusing and coming from the right place, is usually given to aid some destruction, normally to someone terrorising the younger children in the village. When the neighbour's son fell into the river, I think everybody laughed for days. Do you remember, even the vicar gave us a pat on the shoulder as a well done?

Thank you for making the christening gowns. It means so much to Billy and I and you know I was never one for sewing. All that sitting still for long periods of time, setting dainty stiches. I don't know how you can do it. I am going to ignore the fact that you think you are never wrong.

Yes! Father was frantic, looking in all the hedgerows and gardens and wouldn't let us sleep until Patch was found. And then a week later when we camped in the back field of the farm and Father didn't even realise, we had left the cottage. Mother was so angry though when we trooped in at dawn trailing our blankets along in the mud and our nightdresses stained green and covered in hay.

While your classroom numbers have halved, the village school has doubled in children, and I think if we take any more evacuees, then they will have to start sitting on the desks or on the floor.

Give my love to Peggy and Henry.

Your loving sister,

Elizabeth.

Sunday, 18 June 1944

Dear Mother,

Hearing your news of Harry and Henry made me laugh until I couldn't see for tears running down my face. I read your letter during break, and I shared it with Miss Jones, another teacher here, whom I am quite friendly with. We both cackled greatly, only stopping when a small child asked us if we were okay. When I read the first part of the letter, I thought Harry had thrown a piece of chalk at another child, but then my eyes travelled down the page. He threw the chalk back at Jane! That child is possibly the bravest person I have ever met.

Just be thankful, Mother, that Elizabeth and I didn't throw chalk at a teacher. Well, we might have let a few slips but our aim was better, and we were never blamed. Although, you are right, we did cause quite a bit of mischief. You may rest assured that my students now are displaying the same mischievous behaviour which I can do no more than to chuckle at behind my hand.

Thank you for the lace. It is perfect for the gowns. It came yesterday in the evening post. Peggy brought it up for me as the post man had left it by the door.

Love to you all,

Daisy.

Tuesday, 20 June 1944

To my loving wife,

I could see it in your eyes that you were expecting a proposal. I had your sister and mother egging me on though, not to mention my own mother as well. I think you would have been hard pressed to drag me anywhere, me being a six-foot soldier and you being a tiny waif. I jest of course, I would have followed you anywhere. Still would, in fact. My love for you has made me forever yours.

Yes, recalling our evenings spent in one another's company, I don't think your gaze lingered much on my feet. I'll draw them for you if I get a moment, then you can show my monster toe to your students.

I am glad you are having some decent weather; here it is all rain and mud. There is nothing green growing here anymore, and I think we all miss the smell of a crisp summer's day with the smell of summer blooms in the air. I think we all miss any smell that isn't mud, gunpowder, and each other. Still, I am hearing rumours that we are close to winning, and I long for the day when I can hold you in my arms again.

I adore the *Murder on the Orient Express.* My brother and I read it religiously as children. Save it for me, and I will read it when I return home. Oh, what am I saying, you never get rid of books. Unless of course, they are about subjects that you find boring, like gardening! Go and read it, though by the time this letter arrives with you at home, I suspect you will have already finished it twice over.

I am kept on my toes all day and often into the night, tending to wounds and fevers. When I eventually sit in my blanket and close my eyes, all I see is you, my wonderful bride and love of my life. Soon, my dear, I shall be in your arms again, where I belong.

All my love,
Jimmy.

Friday, 23 June 1944

Darling Jimmy,

It is always wonderful to hear from you. I can hear your voice reading your words as though you are sitting next to me, whispering them into my ear. Sometimes, I can even feel the lingering effects of your arms holding me close as we dance into the night.

Please try and complete the drawing of your feet. I shall have to show it to the children at school. They will love it and may encourage them to start drawing themselves. I hope to be nurturing some budding artists!

Jimmy, come home to me soon. Every day, I pray for you, and your fellow soldiers. I pray that you will stay safe and return to me before long. Our time during our courtship was brief but one of the best times of my life, which I wish to continue.

Forever yours,
Daisy.

Monday, 26 June 1944

Dear Elizabeth,

Yes, I heard about what the boys were up to. I think you need to teach them better aim. If they are going to get into trouble, then they might as well make it impressive and worthwhile. Mother definitely wouldn't approve though so it will have to be secret meetings, much like we had with Susan Dooley when we were five.

I had forgotten about our trip to see the stars. We had asked Mother if we could camp out and she said no. So we did the only thing we could do and climbed out of our bedroom window, out onto the tree branch and ran off through the fields. It was worth the wooden spoon against our backsides though. I don't think I could sit right for a week afterwards!

Last week, I found a copy of *Murder on the Orient Express* which I obviously re-read before taking it into school. I am currently reading it to the class, which they are thoroughly enjoying. I think they enjoy the reading almost as much as they enjoy not doing any work. No matter, I think every child should be given plenty of opportunities to read and to fall in love with reading.

Speaking of reading, Peggy reckons that you should read to your unborn child. Apparently, it soothes them, hearing their mother's voice. But maybe start with something light, not your massive engine manuals!

Jimmy's letters are getting fewer and fewer with longer periods of time in between them. Every morning, I meet the postman at the door where he shakes his head sadly before leaving the stack of letters for the rest of my neighbours. I reckon the postman does that in most streets, sadly shaking his head at the lack of news. Or the tearful expression he must don when handing over an official letter or telegram. I thank God every day that I haven't received one of those. I can't even think about what I would do if I received a letter telling me of my husband's death.

The letters I do get, I keep on my mantelpiece, tied together with one of the ribbons held in my hair on my wedding day. Every night, I take them out and re-read them, holding them close to my heart. It is a poor substitute for the real thing, but I can still smell Jimmy on the pages and feel his essence creeping through the lines.

School is helping to take my mind off Jimmy during the day; the children need constant help, support, and attention. They say the best things, mostly without thinking it through first. That's one of the reasons I love teaching, children's ability to cheer you up or make you laugh with such a simple sentence or turn of phrase.

Love to you all,

Daisy.

Thursday, 29 June 1944

Dear Daisy,

Harry's antics are proving to be quite similar to yours and Elizabeth's. I may have to stop him visiting Honeysuckle Cottage. Though, if you put Harry in the war office, we would have this war wrapped up before I could make gravy.

Doesn't your fancy London postman knock on doors? What does he do, throw the parcel out of his basket without stopping? Honestly, you don't get that type of behaviour in Kent. Only yesterday I had a lovely chat with Polly. She's been telling me how she is training up a boy as an apprentice so that she can spend more time with her elderly mother. Yes, dear, you read that right. After dear Harold retired two years ago, we didn't have a man spare, so lovely Polly took up the post. Says it was the best decision she ever made, and she's looking very nice and slim. I feel quite modern having a female postman.

I hope you and Peggy are both well and taking good care of yourselves.

Love,
Mother.

Monday, 3 July 1944

Dear Daisy,

I felt a kick today! I've been feeling little mini kicks but nothing definite. I was getting worried, but then when I woke up in the night, the baby kicked. I woke Billy up in a hurry, grabbing his hand and placing it on my belly. I don't think he realised what was happening until the baby kicked again. Billy fully woke up then. We sat for another ten minutes, both our hands on my belly but the baby had decided that he wanted to go back to sleep. I know it's silly to say he, but in my head, I think it's a boy. Billy thinks I am crazy; no one knows the sex of the baby until its born, but my gut is telling me it's a boy. I gave Billy the same look I gave our teacher when we were thirteen and she told us off for talking through her boring lecture.

Do you know what brought on the baby's movement? That evening, I had started reading to the baby – not one of my engine manuals, although I don't see what is wrong with them. They are very interesting. No, I was reading an old copy of Browning's poems, which the baby seems to like. Billy thinks that it doesn't matter what I read but how I read it. He thinks I could read my ration coupons and the baby wouldn't mind!

I reckon that your class love your reading but are just pretending to be bored. You always had a way with words to

captivate an audience. Jimmy will be back soon; I can feel it in my bones. He is always in our thoughts and prayers.
Stay strong,
Elizabeth.

Saturday, 8 July 1944

Dear Elizabeth,

I am so glad you are finally feeling the baby! It's not long now. When are you doing to take some time off work? If you keep going as you are, you'll deliver surrounded by engine parts. I bet Billy was cowering in his seat after that look. Our teacher certainly never told us off again.

I have a child who acts just like we did when we were at school, and I have since discovered just how much of a pain we were. How did we not end up strung up outside in the school yard?

You have always mocked my love of poetry, but I stand by it, especially if it made the baby respond. Although you will probably say that the baby only kicked to stop you reading. Give my love to Billy and the baby.
Daisy.

Wednesday, 12 July 1944

Dear Mother,

You can't call Polly a postman. And most places have women working men's jobs. Kent needs to catch up with the times.

I can imagine the wrath that would incur when your lavender bush was threatened. Actually, I can remember it from when Elizabeth and I let Patch loose on it and he nearly tore it to shreds. Don't worry, Mother, the war will be over soon, and you can go back to your prize-winning garden.

Peggy and I are doing very well. She is living the high life, married and happy. Henry is such a sweetheart.

Don't let Father grumble too much. You are too soft on him; he should be doing daily exercise, and then he wouldn't grumble so much in the winter.

Love to you all,

Daisy.

Sunday, 16 July 1944

My darling Jimmy,

My mother is moaning about her garden and my father. You would think that there wasn't a war going on and that the biggest issues we faced was which member of the WI was going to win jam week. But there is a war going on. And your absence only highlights that fact.

The children at school are being as lovely as ever. I may change my opinion when we hit the bleaker winter months but for now, they are all being quite nice. I think it may be a fluke because the summer holidays are so close.

Our room is empty and cold without you, despite the heat of the day. I have taken to sleeping in one of your old shirts, the smell of you still lingers on the fabric and it makes me kid myself that you are here with me at night.

Please write soon.
Forever yours,
Daisy.

Thursday, 20 July 1944

Dear Daisy,

Mother would say it serves you right, having a child who behaves as we did. I can't help but admire their bravery though. And I think we narrowly avoided many beatings and punishments by sheer luck!

Harry and Henry have found the joy of reading. They keep coming over to borrow my books and honestly, it is one of the best things I have ever done and encouraged. And I include marrying Billy in that sentence! They were so cute yesterday. They came over and Harry, after finishing *The Velveteen Rabbit,* was mad at the ending. I told him, now he is an official book lover when he gets mad at endings. I know you would be proud. That child has come so far.

I can't wait to see you for a brief time when during your summer holidays, which seems like so long away, but I know it will pass in the blink of an eye.

Do you know when Jimmy is coming home, and for how long? It would be wonderful to see him when he does. We have all missed him.

Elizabeth.

Tuesday, 25 July 1944

Dear Daisy,

Harry and Henry are massively enjoying their time at the village school. Trouble making aside, they are both bright boys. I reckon that they will both go on to be teachers. Harry found your old catapult and is now using it to fling small rocks at passing people and animals. I knew I should have burned that when I had the chance.

People are enjoying the heat of summer, taking the time to take leisurely strolls and picnics by the river. Children have been splashing about in the shallows. It is such a joyous sound to hear. Especially during the bleakness of war.

Are you okay in London? I am hearing more and more reports of London bombings. Are you making sure that you are eating well? And please don't take on any more projects at school. The Easter production strained you to nearly breaking point.

Lots of love,
Mother.

Tuesday, 1 August 1944

Mother, James's home STOP He is well STOP Going back in a week STOP Daisy

---

Wednesday, 9 August 1944

Dear Elizabeth,

This week with Jimmy has been one of the best of my life! I think even better than our wedding day. We have spent the week dancing, talking, laughing, and just spending time in one another's company. It has been blissful, and I cried buckets when I saw him off at the train station. I pray every day for this wretched war to end soon, so that my darling Jimmy will be returned to me.

Jimmy's mother came to visit us as well. It must be hard on her; both her sons are fighting this horrible war, and her husband is dead from the first war. It is hard enough having a loved one across the seas but to have both your children engaged with the war, fighting across Europe.

Please give mother a hug and a kiss from me. I am afraid I sent her a rather snappish telegram, but I was just so eager to be with Jimmy, I think all rational thought escaped my brain. Honestly, the second he stepped off the train, I twirled round him like a May pole without a care to the crowded station or that I attracted many odd stares.

Every day, I woke up in my husband's arms, could bury myself against him. It was blissful.

I feel lighter than air, spending time with my husband has made the world right again.

Much love,

Daisy.

Thursday, 10 August 1944

Dear Mother,

I apologise for the quick and uninformative telegram. I was so excited to see Jimmy home that I couldn't sit still for long enough to write a letter and then walk it down to the post office. I popped into the post office on the way back from the train station where I met Jimmy.

I bet you understand though when father was fighting in the first war. The joy I felt at seeing Jimmy again was indescribable. I felt like I was walking on a cloud. I will try and hold on to this feeling for as long as possible.

I am very glad it is the school holidays; this year has been non-stop and having the week with Jimmy has done wonders for me. I hope you are all doing well.

Love,

Daisy.

Monday, 14 August 1944

Dear Daisy,

I saw the telegram you sent mother. I also saw her reaction. I haven't laughed that much since before the war, so thank you. We were in the post office together when it came through. Mother read it, re-read it, and then glared at the paper as though it were your face. She then passed it to me, saying 'that sister of yours will be the death of me'. Don't worry, she understands what you are going through and understands that you want to spend as much time as possible with Jimmy. I let her come round to Honeysuckle Cottage and rearrange all my cushions and curtains to cheer her up. I had to put everything back to how I like it though after she had left.

You should spend more time with Jimmy's mother. Vera loves it when I pop over for a cup of tea and a chat.
Billy and Bump both doing well.
Elizabeth.

Thursday, 17 August 1944

Dear Elizabeth,

I am glad that I cause you such amusements. I honestly didn't mean to sound rushed or cruel, but there we go. I cannot believe you let her rearrange your cushions! She has been begging to do mine and every time she comes to London, I have to virtually restrain her.

I am having tea with Verity tomorrow. You are right, as always, I should spend more time with her, but these last few months have been hectic, and I have barely had a moment to myself. The children at school are becoming more and more worried about the war and various bombings. Last week we had another child evacuated. At this rate, my class is going to just be me!
Kiss Bump from their auntie.
Daisy.

Saturday, 19 August 1944

Dear Daisy,

Your father says that he has had a bumper crop of potatoes and peas, so he is busy in the fields. Harry and Henry are helping him, having the most fun. They all come back each afternoon full of smiles and giggles – and covered in mud. I cannot begin to tell you how much mud they troop into my freshly polished kitchen every day. Honestly, it is worse than when you and Elizabeth used to come home, trailing grass stains everywhere.

I'll admit, I was a little miffed about the quite-frankly rude telegram. But I do understand why. When your husband comes back on leave, it, at least with me, causes one to act in a way one wouldn't normally. I know it is hard for you, with James being away, either training new medics or working overseas, so I know that the little time you get with him is precious.

I will keep praying that this war will end soon, and then James can come home to you.

Much love,

Mother.

Sunday, 20 August 1944

Darling Jimmy,

Now you are back overseas, I have had a spring clean. Well, I suppose a summer clean, but I felt it needed doing. I found one of your socks under the bed which you must have forgotten to pick up when you were packing to leave again. I'll put it in your drawer. It doesn't have much in, just a few things you can't take with you or spare clothing. Hopefully, the war will end soon, and you can fill it to the brim.

In fact, just last week, I had a letter where mother was complaining about the lavender bush in her garden to the agricultural officer. Of all people to complain to! She is one brave soul.

The week we spent together still lives on in my heart. I can still feel your presence on the sofa, and your smell still lingers on the pillow. I wish for your safe and speedy return; the house is once again empty without you.

All my love,

Daisy.

Saturday, 26 August 1944

Dearest Daisy,

It is hot, so hot here. The smell of blood and wounds isn't great at the best of times, but now it is nearly unbearable. It almost makes me wish for winter when everything gets frozen solid.

I carry our week together always with me. You are the first thing I think of in the morning and the last thing I think of before I go to sleep. You fill every thought; the memory of your laugh brings me joy and the feel of you in my arms helps me to sleep at night.

I have sealed this envelope with a kiss, and the memory of all our time together so far. My darling Daisy, soon I will

hold you in my arms again, which is something that I won't be letting go off in a hurry.
All my love,
Jimmy.

Saturday, 2 September 1944

Darling Jimmy,

The school term has started once again. I said goodbye to some of the older children in July, and I will welcome new arrivals now.

This week has seen the first of the autumn leaves fall off the trees. One fell into my bicycle basket, which I didn't see until I reached home. I have put it on the kitchen windowsill, where I can look at it every day. It remind me of you as it is a gorgeous deep brown, the same colour as your hair.

I have promised the children that when the playground is coated in fallen leaves, I and the other teachers will let them sweep them up into piles so that they can jump in them. It keeps the children happy and means that us teachers don't have to clear the playground.

We've also had the most annoying weather! First, autumn leaves gently falling in a light breeze, then the next day, sheets of rain suddenly descended upon us, soaking everyone. Jimmy, I tell you, even my underwear was soaked through. We were on the playground at the time so the other teachers and I tried to get the children inside but they didn't listen and started running through the drops and splashing each other. We gave up trying to get them inside, they were wet already, and we might as well let them have some fun. I huddled under a small shelter with Miss Jones, each of us trying to keep as dry as possible.

I shall get the children to write poems about it though next week. There is nothing better than using a real experience to help the adjectives flow. And the children are so sick of describing the scenery outside the window.

Forever yours,

Daisy.

Friday, 8 September 1944

Dear Daisy,

Guess what! Old Mrs Ford is moving in with her daughter to help with her children. Penny is now on baby number five and shows no sign of stopping. But that's not the news I wanted to share. Mrs Ford is clearing out her house, so I sent Billy down with our old pulley cart. I've sent Harry and Henry as well; the more people to carry books back the better. I've told him to get anything useful and of course as many books as he can fit in the cart. He asked which books in particular, but I just gave him a look. He knows I would read literally anything. Well nearly anything. Nothing about gardening or knitting.

I was watching out of the window when I saw him coming up the lane, the cart loaded with books and more books in his arms. He had a treasure cove in the cart. There were a few gardening books, but he assures me, they are all for Mother.

Do you remember spending long winter evenings sitting in Mrs Ford's house, reading her books, and begging to borrow them to finish at home? It has brought back so many fond memories, and I know it seems mean to be so happy over an old lady's set of books, but these books bring me back to happier times. Mrs Ford enclosed a note for us. I've copied it out for you.

Dear Elizabeth and Daisy,

The second I decided to move into Penny's house to support her and get rid of most of my things, I knew you would be down here quicker than a knife going through hot butter. I have piled your young man with all your favourites, plus some that you never got round to reading when you were younger. It is a comfort to me to know that my books are going to a good home.

Mrs Ford,

So, I was looking through all the books, thinking I had died and gone to heaven when I came across a copy of *David Copperfield* with a bookmark in. Why would someone start reading one of the greatest works of art of all time and not finish it! I am outraged! It does make me wonder though, could the reader have died, could they have simply run out of time? Billy suggested that the reader had gotten bored, at which I threw a cushion at him.

I have read it now, starting at the beginning and using the bookmark as my own, so now I am sending it to you, alongside a few other books that you will love. I am also sending the bookmark as I feel it belongs with the book. Consider this parcel your Christmas and birthday present.

Much love, your VERY happy sister,
Elizabeth.

Monday, 11 September 1944

Dear Elizabeth,

The books came today. I squealed in excitement, causing Peggy to come out of her flat and into mine because she thought I had fallen and injured myself. Please thank Mrs Ford for me, she always had a warm place in my heart. Well, her library certainly did!

It still baffles me that Billy is not a reader. I think it is his only bad quality. Please make sure my niece or nephew don't inherit this awful trait but grow to love books as much as we did and still do.

I have a child in my class who hates reading. He won't even read his own writing, but I am struggling on with him and by the time he leaves my classroom, he will be a lover of reading. I just need to find the right book for him.

I can't believe that Penny is on baby number five! It seems like yesterday that she was getting married. Although, do you remember, she was already four months pregnant on her wedding day. Her dress could barely fasten up, and I had to sew in another panel into the back.

The leaves have started falling from the trees so next week, the children are going to rake the leaves from the playground. We may jump into the piles we make. I certainly will be. It was one of the best parts of autumn when we were children.

Much love to you all,
Daisy.

Wednesday, 13 September 1944

My darling Jimmy,

Elizabeth has sent me a collection of books she managed to get from a house clearance. The delivery of these books has made me happier than I can describe, and it nearly outshines our wedding day. Nothing could make me happier though than the day we stood in front of friends and family and vowed to love each other until our dying days. Even the war couldn't rear its ugly head that day. I think I must be the luckiest woman in England, marrying such a kind, gentle and loving man. Getting all these books, though is a very close second.

The weather has turned again, and we are now fully approaching winter. It was nice while it lasted, but now the weather has caught up with itself. I don't know what it was hoping to achieve, stretching out the sunshine and making us feel like we had months left of nice weather. Each day, I wrap another scarf round my neck. My students joke that by December, you won't be able to see me, and I'll be more scarf than not. They are only slim scarves, but I read a magazine last year that said many small layers are better than one or two big layers.

The children are not going to like being cooped up inside after a long summer playing outside, running free. We teachers have made a decision that we will try and get them outside whenever we can. I remember when I was a child, my best memories where with Elizabeth, us running through fields, climbing trees and diving into the small river on the outskirts of the village.

Forever yours,

Daisy.

Thursday, 21 September 1944

Dear Daisy,

The child in your class, read to him *The Midnight Folk.* It was the book that got us into reading, the whole mystery and intrigue. Then I can guarantee he will never have his head out of a book. I tried to get Billy into it, but he didn't even open the front cover.

Penny's dress was the biggest scandal the village has ever seen! People were talking about it for months. She still sings your praises though, making sure she was decent to walk down the aisle.

Mother and Father are both doing okay. I know Mother makes Father seem like a grumbling old fool in her letters but since Harry and Henry have come to stay with them, he has been happier and almost younger.

Love,

Elizabeth.

Sunday, 24 September 1944

Dear Daisy,

I have started volunteering my services to the church. It is something that fills my time and gets me out of the house. I really dislike the colder months, little sun, little gardening, and little work. The farm fields have been dug over, ready for a new rotation of crops so as there is only weeding and manual labour jobs to see to; I am really not needed.

Your father and the boys are mending fences next week, checking for holes in cattle fields. Harry is particularly excited about this; he sees it as his duty to guide cattle back into their fields. I know he has visions of chasing hundreds of cows across a lane, and I hate to disillusion him. Bless him.

That David Newton was sent home last week. Haven't seen a peep from his cottage though. I only heard about it because his neighbour was complaining about the noise when I bumped into her in the market. Apparently, the screams can be heard throughout all hours of the night. Your father reckons it is shell shock. I heard from Mrs Grove though that he deliberately let himself get shot so that he could come home.

Stay safe,
Mother.

Wednesday, 27 September 1944

Dear Elizabeth,

I heard from mother about David Newton. Billy and he were friends, weren't they? Maybe he could go over and see him. I've told mother off for gossiping about David though.

He has risked his life for king and country and deserves some respect.

I read *The Midnight Folk* to this boy. He loved it! I don't know why I didn't think of it sooner. His mother came up to me after school and thanked me for helping her child. Apparently, he has come out of his shell, talking more at mealtimes and being nicer to his brothers and sisters. It is always nice to hear from the parents; it makes my work feel meaningful.

I've got to dash. I am writing this letter during my lunch break and any minute now, the headmaster is going to ring the bell letting all the children back inside.

Love to you all,
Daisy.

Saturday, 30 September 1944

Dear Mother,

James always says the war zones are horrible. He says that the soldiers scream all night there, even in the medic tent. James reckons that seeing constant loss around you and hearing the never-ending shells and explosions does no man any favours. Treat poor David with kindness and love and he will hopefully recover soon. You are friends with his mother, why don't you pop round and see what you can do?

I am glad you are volunteering at the church. The vicar should put you to work, dusting everything and reorganising the Bible shelf.

Give Harry and Henry a kiss from me.

Daisy.

Tuesday, 3 October 1944
Dear Daisy,

After church this morning, Billy and I strolled along the river like we were new lovers. The weather may not be as nice as when we first met, but it is blissful to just be in one another's company. I say strolled, but it was more of a waddle on my part and a shuffle on Billy's part. Being pregnant is great and all, but by God I am ready for this baby to come out into the world! Billy is being so kind and lovely. I am, I think, the luckiest girl in the world, marrying such a kind and sweet gentleman.

Billy has been round to David's. He sits and talks to him about work in the factory, me, the baby and how life has been in England since David left. At this stage, I can't say whether or not it is helping or doing any good, but one can only hope. Billy says that David looks happier when he comes. I have also spoken to Mother. She feels rightly ashamed and has resolved to bake David and his mother something nice when she gets the rations.

Work at the factory is going well. I am moving slower, and I have had to move my table further away from my chair, but I am doing very well. It won't be long now before I have to stop working, but I want to continue for a long as I can.
Elizabeth.

Saturday, 7 October 1944

Dear Elizabeth,

I am pregnant! I only found out because on the way to school last week, I slipped on a patch of ice and hit the back of my head. I was near the bakers at the time and the baker's apprentice rushed out and helped me up. I insisted I was fine; I had got in much worse scraps as a child but he said I should go to the doctors just in case. I promised I would.

So, at lunch time, I walked along to the Wednesday clinic and one of the nurses examined me. She said I was looking very pale and to be safe, she wanted to do a test. The results came back yesterday, and I am pregnant! I just wish Jimmy were here to share in my joy.

Happy mother-to-be,

Daisy.

Saturday, 7 October 1944

Darling Jimmy,

I have wonderful news. I am pregnant! It is our little miracle, my little keep-sake from our week together over the summer. It is still early days, but I am so incredibly happy.

I haven't heard from you in several weeks. Please tell me you are safe and that the reason for your silence is an abundance of injured men needing your attention. It would be wonderful to have you home for the birth of your son or daughter.

Forever yours,

Daisy.

Saturday, 7 October 1944
Dear Mother and Father,

I know that by November you will be grandparents and I am adding to that. By May you will be grandparents again. I am expecting! The nurses did the test last week. I am so happy I could dance through the streets!

I have written to Jimmy, expressing our joyous news. Hopefully, he writes back soon, or even better, comes home in time to see the birth of his son or daughter.

Love and kisses to you all.

Daisy.

Monday, 9 October 1944

Dear Daisy, Happy birthday! 21 at last.

Harry and Henry drew me the cutest picture, which I have propped up on the mantle top. They came to the cottage door and presented it to me along with a bunch of flowers they found at the side of the lane.

What wonderful news! I bet you and Jimmy are thrilled. Have you written to him? Has he replied yet? I knew it would happen soon. Whenever Jimmy is home, you two can't seem to keep your hands off each other.

Billy is going to post this for me as I am now on ordered bed rest from the nurse. I told her that we are in the middle of a war and that I need to be at work, but she just tutted and said I wasn't to get out of bed for anything other than to use the privy.

I am going to get so bored, cooped up here all day and all night. I might try and sneak off.

Love,

Elizabeth.

P.S. Don't listen to your sister. She will be fine. I may have to tie her down to the bed if she keeps trying to get up though. The nurse said everything is fine and that Elizabeth and baby are looking as healthy as can be. Billy.

Tuesday, 10 October 1944

Dear Elizabeth,

Firstly, happy birthday to you as well. Secondly, listen to Billy and the nurse. The nurse has probably seen millions of babies enter this world, so she knows what she is doing. They only have your health in mind. Peggy agrees with me, and she reckons you should have stopped working in the summer. I told her that you were as stubborn as a mule. I had visions of you popping out a baby surrounded by spanners, coils, and grease.

I think when I come towards the end of my own pregnancy, I will be as bored as you are now. I am just telling myself that I can spend the day reading, without a care in the world.

I am attempting to grow my own flowers in a window box, but I think all I am managing so far is a pot of earth. I should have paid attention to mother's gardening books instead of just burying them in the garden or throwing them down the well. I might just give up on the flowers and grow carrots or potatoes. At least they are easy to grow and don't need much expertise.

Give Billy a big kiss from me. He doesn't deserve you, he is too nice.
Daisy.

Thursday, 12 October 1944

Dear Daisy,

I hope you had a good birthday celebration. I went over to your sisters for tea and feel bad that I can't come down to London what with the bombings and such. As soon as this wretched war is over, you and I shall have to do something special.

The news of another addition to our family makes my heart want to burst from joy. I wish I could have had more children, but God only granted me two. Although, I didn't think you would turn out to be twins, so I suppose I got two for the price of one. We all hope and pray that James will be home before the birth. To look into your child's new-born face is one of the best parts about being a parent.

Harry and Henry are as happy as two young boys are at the news of a baby coming. Every time they go and visit Elizabeth, they poke her stomach and ask if the baby is ready yet. God bless those sweet boys.

Your father is grumbling again, the change of seasons was never kind to him. He is just not a cold weather person. I've moved his chair into the kitchen where he can sit closer to the oven. He puts his feet up on the open oven door though, which I wish he wouldn't do. Those socks, no matter how much I wash them, are always filthy. I blame it all on your father pottering round the garden with no shoes on.

I've just turned the garden over so that the soil is ready for planting come the spring, leaving the potatoes and various vegetables where they are. Oh, the day when I can go back to growing prize worthy roses, gardenias, and dancing ladies. I was allowed to keep my big lavender bush, which as I told the agricultural officer, was good because otherwise I would have to rename the cottage and then the postman would get all confused. I told him that bush has been there since before the great war, and it certainly isn't coming down now. He backed off, looking a bit faint. Your father reckons I have scared him off. Well, I said, good riddance to him then!

I worry about you in London, all that bombing, especially now you're with child. Is it worth you coming back home, at least until you have the baby?

Love and kisses,

Mother.

Monday, 16 October 1944

My darling Jimmy,

We were writing poems in class today, and I wanted to write a short poem for you, something to express how much I love you, but I couldn't think of words worthy enough. So, I am settling with this letter, saying how much I miss you, and how much me and our unborn child wish you were home with us.

The baby is due to arrive in May, but Peggy reckons it will come nearer to the end of April. Hopefully by then, this war will be over, and you will have returned to us.

Forever yours,
Daisy.

Tuesday, 17 October 1944

Dear Daisy,

The nurse seeing to me is none other than Nurse Maude, the same woman who helped mother deliver us all those years ago. She is still the same as ever, insisting on proper behaviour and everything by the book. I wish I had one of the younger nurses; they seem kinder. Although I think that Nurse Maude is only like that because of how we used to pull her washing off the line.

As I told the nurse, there is a war going on and every pair of hands is needed, especially since we have sent most of our young men overseas. Besides, I can't see you giving up work months before you have to. You'll be giving birth surrounded by lots of other children! Or maybe you'll get lucky and time it well for lunchtime. Wouldn't that be something! If that happens, it had better get into the newspapers.

I have just laughed so hard at the thought. The baby is joining my mirth and is showing its appreciation by kicking my bladder.

I am reading. Lots! I have a stack of books that I am working my way through. I keep sending Billy out for more, and I think one day he is going to just throw them at me from the bedroom door.

Girls from the factory keep popping in so it is like a circus in here, and I have drunk more cups of tea than I can count. This baby is honestly going to come out looking like a tea leaf.

Please give up growing flowers. You know what happened last time. Billy agrees with me, he says he can't cope with another vine explosion like the one in '42!

I hope you and Peggy are doing okay.
Elizabeth.

Friday, 20 October 1944

Dear Elizabeth,

Peggy has been moved from the hospital to district nursing. She doesn't mind, says it broadens her knowledge, and she gets the opportunity to help those who can't afford or can't get to the hospital. Her mother on the other hand is not happy. She has taken the view that district nursing is for commoners and that Peggy will die of a hundred horrible diseases before the day is out. When Peggy told me this, I laughed for hours. I promised her to write to her mother in the event of her death from 'a hundred horrible diseases'. Peggy just hit me with a rolled-up magazine, laughing.

I remember Nurse Maude; she was the one who always patched us up when we got ourselves into scrapes. I have lost count of the number of times she sighed, rolled her eyes, and then proceeded to lecture us on why we shouldn't climb trees or jump over rivers. But she always gave us a pear drop or a barley sugar afterwards.

I have taken your advice and Billy's fear, and I've planted some potatoes. They may not grow bigger than a sixpence, but at least I have tried.

Yesterday, I met up with Verity. She was delighted about the news of another grandchild. Jimmy's brother, Michael, has got a bouncing baby girl who I nearly put in my handbag to take home with me, last time I saw them all. That was before finding out about my own pregnancy, of course.

Jimmy hasn't written back yet. I have never been this long without some form of contact from him. At this point, I would take the shortest letter from Jimmy, even a telegram will do. I just want something to reassure me that he is okay.

Write soon,

Daisy.

Monday, 23 October 1944

Dear Mother,

I have enclosed three hats, one each for the boys and one for Father. The bigger one is for father and the boys can chose amongst the other two. Peggy and I celebrated my birthday with Horlicks and gossip, which given the war and our hectic working schedules, was perfect and just the right tonic for all the depression and uncertainty ruling our lives.

The bombings have been frequent, but we all get to the air raid shelters in plenty of time. I think the Nazis are hitting churches and other important buildings, so we are not being targeted much. I am safe here; I would prefer to stay in London and keep teaching for as long as possible. Give Harry and Henry a kiss and a cuddle from me.
Daisy.

Wednesday, 25 October 1944

Dear Mrs James Fitz,

I am sorry to write this letter. It is not one I look forward to writing. Your husband, Doctor J Fitz, has been declared Missing in Action (MIA) on 5 October 1944.

My thoughts and prayers are with you in this sad time.
Captain P Goode.

Thursday, 2 November 1944

Dear Mother,

I know it has only been a short time since my last letter, but Jimmy has been declared missing. I had a letter from his captain a few days ago. He can't be missing. What does that even mean? Is he dead? He wasn't supposed to be on the front lines, just in the medic's tent. What if he dies? What if he dies

before knowing our child? I don't even know if he knows I am pregnant. What am I going to do? Peggy has slept over for the last couple of nights, which has been a great help. Being alone right now just doesn't seem like something I can do. Although, I guess I will never be alone, not with Jimmy's child growing inside me.
Daisy.

Friday, 3 November 1944

Dear Daisy,

I am going to come and stay with you for a bit. I think you need some company. Your father agrees with me and is happy to look after the boys for a week or so.
Mother.

Sunday, 5 November 1944

Dear Daisy,

First of all, tell Peggy to go for it. She should do what makes her happy and what best helps the war effort. District nursing is no more dangerous than any other job we women are picking up to help out.

Secondly, Mother told me about Jimmy. She didn't want to at first, but I wheedled it out of her. Just because Jimmy is missing, doesn't mean he is dead. You must keep hope that he will return.

If you need anything, please write, or come and visit. You know I am always here for you, whatever you need. Also, please make sure you take care of yourself, if not for your sake, then for your baby's.

Our thoughts and prayers are with you.
Elizabeth and Billy.

Wednesday, 8 November 1944

Dear Elizabeth,

I arrived in London yesterday evening. I have spoken to Peggy, who assures me that she has been keeping a medical and a friendly eye on Daisy. I could do no more than hug the lovely girl. Daisy is…well, I can't describe it. She is like a thinner, paler version of herself. When she opened her door to me, she just launched herself at me, crying and crying. I've never seen her so broken. She and you have always been strong beacons of light, charging forward without a care in the world.

Daisy is still going to school, which I am grateful for, as she seems to throw herself into her work, which seems to be helping with the pain.

Keep writing to her, Elizabeth, she needs to hear from you. I am going to stay for as long as I can. Keep yourself well rested and don't do anything that might harm your baby. I know you are distressed for your sister, but you also need to think of yourself in this situation.

Please send Billy to check on your father and the boys.
Mother.

Saturday, 11 November 1944
Dear Daisy,

Jimmy will be home soon; I can feel it. Please don't lose hope.

Your loving sister,
Elizabeth.

Monday, 13 November 1944

Dear Peggy,

How is Daisy doing? I know our mother is staying with her, but I want to hear from you too. Is she feeding herself and taking care of herself? I would come down to London, but the nurse has ordered me on bed rest. She is not replying to my letters, and I just need the reassurance that she is doing okay.

I am going out of my mind here in bed. All I want to do is go outside, go work on an engine, anything that doesn't involve me lying in this bed. Billy thinks I am going to sneak out, and I am tempted…so, tempted.

How are you and Henry doing? I heard about your move to district nursing, and I think it is amazing. You are out there in the community, helping people. Don't listen to a word your mother says.

Elizabeth.

Thursday, 16 November 1944

Dear Elizabeth,

Thank you for your kind words about my transfer to district nursing. Henry says the same thing about my mother, telling me I should just ignore her. So, I am throwing all my energy into my work and making sure Daisy is okay.

Your sister is doing as well as can be expected. She is eating enough to keep her and the baby going. She is also still going to school, which I think is doing her a world of good. The children are a natural tonic to most things and Daisy comes back each day with a ghost of a smile on her face.

You should definitely listen to your nurse. If you were one of my patients, I think I would have throttled you by now. Keep resting, you only have a few more weeks left. And then you won't want to do anything! The baby will keep you awake at odd hours and will need constant attention. But a baby is one of the best things in this world.

Daisy is reading your letters even if she doesn't have the energy to respond. They are bringing her comfort.

Henry is being such a rock throughout all of this. He has stayed by my side through my mother, me helping Daisy and everything life seems to throw at us.

Keep safe.
Peggy.

Tuesday, 21 November 1944

Jimmy,

Where are you? Please come home. Our child grows bigger every day, and my belly is starting to show through my blouse. How I wish that you were home to wrap your strong hands round me, holding me and your babe safe in your arms. Jimmy…

I want you home.

Please.

Sunday, 3 December 1944

Dear Daisy,

Yesterday I gave birth to a smiling baby boy – and an adorable baby girl.

I know they are early, but the nurse said they were early as they are twins and that they were ready to come out into the world now.

So, you were right, it was twins. We have named the boy Keith after our father and the girl Vera after Billy's mother. Both are happy and healthy, and Billy is besotted with them. I think they will grow up with him wrapped round their little fingers.

The nurse pops round every day to check mine and the babies' progress. Everything is healthy and normal. I cannot get over how cute and tiny they are. When Billy comes home from work, he scoops up first one baby and then the other. He is so sweet with them, laying with them on the rug and playing with their tiny toes.

A very tired new mother,
Elizabeth.

Wednesday, 6 December 1944

Dear Elizabeth,

I am so happy for you and Billy. I look forward to visiting when my own baby is born. The news of the birth of your twins has lightened my life considerably and it gives me hope that this world is good.

Having mother here has helped me through some dark days, but I am sending her back now as I think you need her more than I do.

Love,
Daisy.

Saturday, 10 December 1944

Dear Daisy,

Firstly, my Christmas rose has bloomed. Someone needs to tell it that it isn't Christmas yet. It does this every year, despite me putting a calendar next to the pot and talking to it every day, it still insists on blooming nearly a month early. Your father thinks I am quite mad, but then he chats to his vegetables, so he isn't one to talk. My mother taught me that plants grow better when they feel loved and cherished, so that's what I am doing. She made no mention of vegetables though, which in my opinion grow whether you talk to them or not.

Secondly, after returning to Kent, I wanted to do something for you to bring you even a small amount of comfort. So, I dug out the letter James sent me and your father when he asked for our blessing to ask you to marry him. I have copied it out for you.

Dear Mr and Mrs Franklin,

My name is Doctor James Fitz, and I have been courting your daughter, Daisy. We met in London, at a soldier's dance, where she swept me off my feet. I know this has been a whirlwind courtship, but I love your daughter with all my heart and even though I am just a humble doctor, I will provide Daisy with a full and happy life. I love her so much, which is why I am asking for your blessing to ask for her hand in marriage. Daisy is the light of my life and the reason I wake smiling every morning.

Yours sincerely,

James Fitz.

Our response was that we would be happy to welcome him into the family and couldn't wait to meet him. I hope this letter brings you some small measure of comfort, seeing how much James loves you. I believe in my soul that he is still alive and is fighting tooth and nail to come home to you and the baby.

Love,

Mother.

Thursday, 14 December 1944
Jimmy,

The days are blurring together. The only saving grace is school and the children. I don't know what I would do without them. Jimmy, I need you to come home to me. I need you. Our baby needs you …

I lay awake most nights, thinking of you. I wish we had met earlier, so that we could have had longer time together. I wish you hadn't gone …

Christmas is coming nearer, and I don't know how I can celebrate it without you here. Oh, to have you here where we could stroll along in the park or even just to sit together on the sofa in each other's arms. I just want time to speed up to when you are returned home safely to me.

Jimmy …

Your mother called round today. I forgot in my grief that she has also lost her son. She persuaded me to take a walk out with her in the park. I must admit it was nice to go outside and feel the cold breeze on my face. We are having surprisingly good weather for the time of year, but it isn't fair, not when you aren't here to enjoy it with me.

It is Christmas. Last year we were barely courting, and you had to leave before we could spend the day together. I had hoped that this year we would have been able to spend it together. Maybe next year …

Today I felt the baby kick. I think it's a boy. I did my gran's old trick of waving a ring over my stomach and I think it is a boy. A little boy with your dark hair and beautiful eyes would be amazing. My mother thinks I shouldn't put all my faith in an old gypsy trick, but I can feel it. A mother knows these things.

Jimmy, please return back to me. I can't stand these cold, lonely nights without you.

Wednesday, 10 January 1945

Dear Daisy,

Please respond to our letters. We just want you to be okay. You are more than welcome to come and stay with us for as long as you want. Stay strong and keep faith, Jimmy will come home.
Love,
Mother.

Saturday, 13 January 1945

Dear Daisy,

The twins are so cute. Yesterday, Vera giggled when Billy made funny faces. I was right about Billy and fatherhood. He has taken to it like a polar bear to ice. And the twins have him wrapped round their little fingers. Thank you for the christening gowns. Turns out I did need both! I'll save them for you though, for your new arrival later on in the year. We are holding the christening next week on the 21st. If you want to come, then you will always be welcome. It might be good for you, and then you could meet your new niece and nephew. I understand how hard these last few months have been for you. You have been amazingly strong and brave.

Your loving sister,
Elizabeth.

Tuesday, 16 January 1945

Dear Peggy,

I thank you again for keeping an eye on my sister. Your friendship, especially these last few months, has been invaluable. To us all. Speaking of Daisy, how is she? How is the baby doing?

We are holding a christening service for Vera and Keith this Sunday. Billy and I would love it if you and Henry could come. Could you try and persuade Daisy to come too? Maybe you could all get the train down together. I have written to Daisy asking her as well, but I am not expecting a reply. I think that she needs to start grieving and only she can decide how and when she does that. I hope to see you on Sunday.
Elizabeth.

Thursday, 18 January 1945

Dear Elizabeth,

Henry and I will be delighted to come. We both have the day off anyway. I was going to risk a visit to my mother, but I would much rather come and spend the day in Kent. I have spoken to Daisy. I think she is going to come too. We will get the early train, but we both have to be back in London Sunday evening for work on Monday. Her face did light up at the mention of the twins, so I know she is looking forward to meeting her niece and nephew. Daisy has been writing to Jimmy, long pieces of paper with ramblings and odd sentences. She hasn't sent any of them. I don't know who they would go to anyway, but I think writing to Jimmy is a coping mechanism for her. Sort of like a diary. I have asked Matron to put me on as her nurse during her pregnancy. I explained the situation to her, and she agreed. So, I pop in everyday, listen to the baby's heartbeat and take Daisy's pulse and temperature. Both are doing very well and in no time at all, we will have a cute little baby in our midst. See you on Sunday.

Peggy.

Monday, 22 January 1945

Jimmy,

Yesterday was Keith and Vera's christening. They looked so cute in their gowns, being held by Billy and Elizabeth.

Peggy, Henry, and I went down to Kent on the early train yesterday. I was glad for their company, but I would have rather had you by my side.

Thursday, 25 January 1945

Dear Daisy,

It was wonderful to see you on Sunday. I know that Elizabeth and William really appreciated your presence.

Aren't the babies just adorable! Your face came alive when you held baby Vera. It is a look I haven't seen in a long time on you. Remember that feeling and hold it close when you have darker days.

Harry and Henry were delighted to see you, and I am glad you spent time with them. They are honestly a balm for the soul despite the trouble they cause for me and the school. Your father sends his love.
Mother.

Wednesday, 31 January 1945

Dear Elizabeth,

Thank you for inviting me to the christening, it has made me smile once more, seeing my niece and nephew. Seeing you so happy with them. It was good to get out of London as well.

Please, can you keep writing to me? Your letters bring me joy and comfort I didn't think I could feel without Jimmy here.
Daisy.

Saturday, 3 February 1945

Jimmy,

Where are you? I need you! Please come back to me.
Our baby needs you.
I am so tempted to march overseas and find you myself.

Saturday, 3 February 1945

Dear Daisy,

It is wonderful to see a letter appear from you. On Monday I am going back to work. I can't believe how much I have missed it. Obviously, I am going to miss the twins like crazy, but I need to get back to work, especially after the months of bed rest. Mother is going to take care of the babies during the day, and I know that they will be in the best hands. Billy wants me to take more time, but I am ready. Besides, I am only going back a couple of days a week.

I've found our copy of *Wuthering Heights* at the back of mother's wardrobe. I am sending it to you. I could never get through it, but I know it is one of your favourites. I can't believe she had it there for so long! Can you imagine what other treasures she is hiding there? I am going to ask her to sort out her wardrobe and see if there is any more of our old books stashed away.

Happy reading,
Elizabeth.

Wednesday, 7 February 1945

Jimmy,

Elizabeth sent me my old copy of *Wuthering Heights*. I had forgotten how much I enjoyed reading it when I was a teenager. I think I read it every week and had to tie it together with an old set of shoelaces, it got so battered and worn.

Friday, 9 February 1945

Dear Daisy,

Being back at the factory is fabulous. The girls have all welcomed me back into the fold, asking about the twins. After the war, I have decided, I am going to continue working. The extra income is always appreciated, especially now that we have two babies instead of one to feed and clothe. Money aside, I have found my passion in life. Apart from my family, nothing brings me greater joy than mending an engine part or getting covered in grease.

It's not long now until you will have your own baby. I am going to repay what you said to me, you could be having twins. Everyone scoffed at your suggestion that I was carrying twins, but their tune changed when two babies popped out. Twins do run in our family, so it might be a possibility. Did you try Gran's ring trick? Looking back, I think the reason mine couldn't settle on a direction, was because there was one of each in there.

Please write to me soon, I miss reading about the school, the baby and life in London in general.
Much love,
Elizabeth.

Sunday, 18 February 1945

Dear Daisy,

I feel young again, looking after two bouncing babies. It feels like when I held you and your sister in my arms, played with you and laid you down in your shared crib. We tried two separate cribs but both of you would yell and scream until you were put together. And then you both laid down peacefully and slept all night. In fact, even when you had separate rooms, I would still find one of you in the other's room. I know you think you were being sneaky and quiet, but me and your father knew. We thought it was sweet. I have a feeling Vera and Keith are going to be like that.

How is school going? And the children? I imagine it won't be long before you have to stop working for the baby. Would you like to come down to Kent when you do finish? You would be welcome any time. Let me know what you decide.
Love,
Mother.

Tuesday, 20 February 1945

Jimmy,

What do I do? I need you to be home for the baby. I have had dreams of you coming home to me where we could just spend our days walking along the river, hand in hand; just the two of us – well, just the three of us.

Come home to me, my sweet Jimmy.

Saturday, 24 February 1945

Dear Daisy,

Tomorrow is mother and father's wedding anniversary. I have the day off work, so I am looking after the twins and Harry and Henry. Father has planned a surprise picnic for her at the meadow where he proposed. Isn't that sweet? I hope that when Billy and I reach twenty-five years of marriage, he will still sweep me off my feet with surprises.

The plan is for me to walk round at 11 o'clock and pick up the boys. My excuse is that mother needs a break, so I will take the boys. Then father will take mother out for a walk, taking her to their spot where a picnic will be already laid out.

Billy and I are going to take the boys and the twins to the lake and let them go swimming. Remember when we were kids and that horrible boy dared us to jump in, not thinking we would do it? Oh, the look on his face when we did! I just can't believe I ended up marrying him! Billy, looking over my shoulder as I write this, has just rolled his eyes! He says that he only dared us to jump because he wanted an excuse to talk to me. He is such a sweetheart.

Love and kisses to you, my gorgeous sister.
Elizabeth.

Thursday, 1 March 1945

Jimmy,

Even though I know you are missing and unlikely to return to my waiting embrace, I find it a comfort to write these unsent letters. It helps me to hold you close to me, no matter how far away you are.

I am now on maternity leave. I said my goodbyes to the children. We all cried a bit, but I told them I would be back before they know it.

Sunday, *4 March 1945*

Dear Daisy,

Visiting my mother has brought me no joy. In fact, I think it has sucked all remaining joy from the world. I have only been here for a few hours, but already I have been lectured on my job, my patients, you, Henry, London, the bombings, my lack of 'nice' clothes and the lack of a child despite having been married for months now. Can you believe that? She doesn't even approve or support my marriage to Henry but has the audacity to ask about children! I have just been answering questions, trying not to incur my mother's wrath too much.

I managed to escape through to the servants' quarters where I am currently writing this letter. Everyone down here was always so much nicer to me when I was growing up. I have even managed to scrounge an apple tart. It is like the war hasn't even touched my mother. She has the barest of rationing and hasn't given up Chiswick House to be used as a soldier's home for recuperation. I think the only concession she has made is to reduce the staff down from four footmen to two and has halved the number of maids. Even that she says she can't cope and that the house is falling into disrepair.

I am being held here until Tuesday so I will see you then. If you need anything, Henry couldn't make the trip, lucky bugger, so just knock, and he will be there.

Peggy.

Friday, 9 March 1945

Dear Daisy,

Last week, your father surprised me by taking me for a glorious picnic in the spot where he had proposed. I didn't think he still had it in him to be romantic and sweet. Elizabeth wandered round to collect the boys and then your father appears at the kitchen door saying we should take a stroll along the river. I agreed, having already scrubbed the steps and hung out the washing.

And then we made it past the trees and spread out on the grass bank was a picnic basket sitting on top of my best tablecloth. We'll be having words about that later; it takes days to clean that properly, and I only bring it out for the best company like the vicar. Or if we get a royal visit.

So, we sat, your father had made sandwiches and brought a small pie from the shop. Oh Daisy, I felt like so young again, like I was newly engaged, looking forward to my life with my new husband.

Walked back to the cottage to find Elizabeth, the boys and the twins awaiting our arrival. Henry had plucked a small bunch of flowers for me. From my own garden, ripped out by their stems and not dug out by the roots but the thought was there. Your father started laughing but had enough good sense to try and hide it with a cough.

I have put the tablecloth into soak and for the next few days, I shall be concentrating on trying to remove the grass stains.

Much love,

Mother.

Sunday, 11 March 1945

Dear Daisy,

How are you and the baby doing? I wish we had twin telepathy like we used to tell everyone we had. It would be great to peer inside your brain so that I knew you were okay.

I've just tried concentrating really hard, but we must just be too far away. Billy laughed and said my face looked like I was trying to pass wind. I have simply thrown my book at him. Now he is keeping it ransom until I give him a kiss. I'm going to finish my letter to you first, let him stew for a bit.

School finished a week early here, much to the children and teacher's delight – and much to the parent's disappointment. Mother is going to send Harry and Henry out with father every day, her reasoning being, 'I remember what you and your sister were like, stamping mud in every time I had cleaned the floor, those boys can spend the majority of the Easter holidays outside, only coming in once they have no traces of mud on them.' Mother used to get so cross when we came in dirty on washing day. Remember the time she got so cross, she wacked us both round the buttocks with her dish towel, meaning we couldn't sit right for a few days?

Billy has suggested a camping trip to the hidden meadow where we all used to go as kids. Harry is very keen on this idea just so long as there are no adults. He wanted to take the twins, but I told him that they were too young so maybe next year. Gosh, I hope they still aren't here next year. Not because they are horrible children, just that I hope the war would have ended before that.

You and Jimmy continue to be in everyone's thoughts and prayers.
Elizabeth.

Wednesday, 14 March 1945

Dear Elizabeth,

Daisy has been put on official bed rest. She wanted to finish the term at school, but it is only another week anyway, so I put my foot down. I didn't want to; school and the children were keeping her mind occupied but as I said, term is finishing soon anyway so she would have to have stopped at some point.

Last night we had another air raid. Neither Daisy nor I were working, so we ran down to the shelter together. Well Daisy ran as much as a seven-month pregnant woman can run. Once settled, we leant back on the wall to wait it out. There isn't much to do when the siren goes off. Just a lot of sitting and waiting. Sometimes someone brings a book they were reading before the sirens went off and didn't have time to put down. Last night, our neighbour hadn't let go of his book so his mother asked if she could read it out loud to us all. We all nodded blearily, anything to pass the time and not think of what damage and destruction is going on above our heads.

So, this boy gave his book to his mother, and she started reading aloud from the beginning. Elizabeth, I am more worried for Daisy than I have ever been, she only paid the barest attention to the story despite it being one on her own shelf. I thought the book might bring her some comfort, but she just sat stroking her stomach, starring at a spot on the wall opposite us.

Other than this, Daisy and baby are healthy. Daisy is eating just enough to keep the baby happy and kicking. She is clinging to the fact that the baby will be a part of Jimmy, and she takes comfort in the fact that she hasn't lost him entirely. Give my best to your parents and give the twins a big cuddle from Daisy and me.

Peggy.

Friday, 16 March 1945

Jimmy,

I am on bed rest. I can hear your laughter in my mind, telling me to behave for the nurses and that you would be glad of bed rest. I can also imagine your arms around me, making my confinement so much easier, reading to me, bringing me cups of tea, and massaging my swollen ankles. Instead, I have Peggy, who is lovely, but she's just not you.

Monday, 19 March 1945

Dear Peggy,

I can't put into words how grateful that we all are that you and Daisy became such good friends. I know Mother doesn't feel right about leaving her in London alone, but knowing you are there, is a balm on us all.

I am glad Daisy is on bed rest, although I suspect she didn't go willingly. Me and her are too much alike, much to our mother's disappointment, and neither of us like to be told to lay in bed for a few weeks. Just ask Billy, I was a nightmare in my final month. I think he contemplated sleeping in the garden, and the ground was frozen solid!

If books aren't bringing her out of this shell, she has put herself in, then we can only hope that the birth of her child will. Maybe seeing the baby and having another tiny human being to take care of will snap her out of her daze. I know all this comes across as very harsh, but I say it with love.

I did suggest to her the same thing she suggested to me during my pregnancy, that she may be carrying twins. Our family has a history of twins, including our father. As her nurse, I know there isn't anything you can do to check, but maybe you could gently broach the subject with her. Maybe start preparing her for it. I know it was a shock to me when two babies came out instead of one.

Much love,

Elizabeth.

Thursday, 22 March 1945

Dear Daisy,

I hope you are sticking to that bed rest the nurse put you on. Your sister was constantly moaning over the lack of things to do, and I once caught her sneaking out of bed. God knows where she was going. I put a swift stop to that. Honestly, when I was pregnant with the two of you, I was a model patient. Just ask any of the older nurses.

Do you want me to come and stay again? I could stay for the baby's birth and a little after to help you get back on your feet. Your father wouldn't mind. Last time, he and the boys spent the whole week outside, only venturing in briefly for food. They even slept outside, although God knows it must have been freezing. I have no sympathy for any of them.

Let me know about coming to London, I can be there within the day.

Mother.

Sunday, 25 March 1945

Dear Daisy,

Don't listen to a word your mother says. She was just like Elizabeth, and I guess you, complaining about bed rest, complaining about not allowed to leave the house and moaning how the nurses trooped in and out without a care for her floors. Just complaining about everything. She even started throwing items at me when I suggested that because I was a twin myself, she might be carrying twins. After you girls were born, I had an 'I told you so' all lined up but then I saw your beautiful faces, cradled in your mother's arms, and I had no words left in me. At this point, I thanked God that I had two beautiful, healthy children and I haven't brought up that conversation again.

Your mother was, I think, one of the worst patients in the village, and I apologised to the nurses every time they came for her check-ups.

She would come and stay with you in London if you need her. She forgets that I am not an old man, incapable of anything. It's completely up to you, although I understand your lovely neighbour has been taking quite excellent care of you.

I know I don't often write, letting your mother talk and talk for as long as she can hold a pencil, but I thought you could do with some kind words without the hysteria of your mother.

Soon your baby will be born, and you will be able to hold your child in your arms and there is nothing better than that. Holding a tiny person, a mirror image of you and the one you love, no other feeling compares. Stay strong, Jimmy will be back before you know it.
Father.

Tuesday, 27 March 1945

Jimmy,

The baby is kicking all night. He just wants to come out into the world to play. Please come home, Jimmy, my love, to hold our baby and watch him grow.

I had a rare letter from my father which helped to focus my thoughts. My mother so often writes for both of them that I forget how kind and gentle my father is.

Friday, 30 March 1945

Dear Daisy,

I have practically had to tie mother up to stop her jumping on the next train to London. I told her that if you wanted someone to stay, you or Peggy would have written to ask one of us to. Between you and me, I was quite glad she went to stay in London with you. Left me a bit of peace and quiet. I can imagine that the nurses would have shooed her out anyway. You know how much of a busy body she can be at times. Besides, the flat would just be too crowded, what with hundreds of nurses all trooping in and out, poking you and examining you from all angles.

She packed a bag the second she got home from posting her last letter to you. Father quietly unpacked it while she was out yesterday. We have both talked her into staying here until she hears word from you.

I am counting down the days until you deliver. Mother thinks end of April, and I reckon it'll be early May. Billy and father are not submitting a guess, having no desire to 'interfere' in woman's problems.

I've enclosed the beautiful christening gowns you made for the twins. I don't know if you will need one or both, but I thought I would save on postage.

Love,

Elizabeth.

Monday, 2 April 1945

Dear Elizabeth,

Daisy's due date gets nearer and nearer. She showed me your last letter. I have to agree with you, Elizabeth, I think she will deliver at the beginning of May. Daisy's other midwife says that we shouldn't bet on when babies arrive and that they will arrive when they are good and ready. I just rolled my eyes. She is of the older persuasion, thinking that midwifery has to be done a certain way.

If you are anything like Daisy, then I can fully imagine what you were like. In fact, my sympathies are lying fully with Billy.

The three of us went to church this morning, walking along in the sunshine afterwards. Henry had to go off to work soon after the service, so Daisy and I linked arms and walked back home. It was lovely, feeling the sun on our faces and seeing the flowers everywhere we looked. We are all good here in London.

Peggy and Daisy.

Thursday, 5 April 1945

Jimmy,

Sometimes I forget that you won't be responding to these letters, not just because I haven't sent them but because you …

I can't bring myself to even write the words, let alone say them out loud.

I am talking to the baby, telling tales of his brave and wonderful father. I have spoken of our wedding, our courtship, and our love affair across the seas. At my voice, the baby moves or kicks. He likes hearing about his father, and he and I both implore you to come home soon so that you can fully meet your wonderful child.

Monday, 9 April 1945

Dear Elizabeth,

Thank you for all your letters. I know I have been a terrible sister and daughter to have not written back, especially when you all have been such a comfort to me these last couple of months. I also know that you and Peggy have been writing to each other these last few weeks, her giving you updates on the baby. I keep feeling the baby moving, kicking away. I have a gut feeling that it is a boy, he will be running havoc all over the streets of London soon. The thought of twins did enter my mind but, in my head, this is one baby, a boy with his father's hair and kind brown eyes. Thank you for the gowns. In my mind, Jimmy would be here

to collect the parcel and hold one over my stomach as if trying it on for size. Or holding one in his arms, practicing for when our baby sits there instead. Bed rest is dragging. I just wish for Jimmy to return home in time for the baby's birth.
Love always,
Daisy.

Thursday, 12 April 1945

Dear Mother,

Every day the baby gets more and more active. I have taken to singing to him, slow dancing around the kitchen. Sometimes I feel ghost arms around me, Jimmy holding me and our child as we sway together, bringing with it, memories of all the times spent in his arms.

Thank you for the offer to come and stay. In truth, it would be very cramped. I was grateful for your company in November, it pulled me through what was, I think, the darkest period of my life. Hearing the news that Jimmy was missing in action nearly killed me, and the only thing to keep me going was the thought of a mini-Jimmy growing inside me. Peggy and my other nurse, Alice, will take good care of me. The only other person I wish to be in the room would be Jimmy, and I pray every day that he comes home in time.
Daisy.

Saturday, 14 April 1945

Dear Daisy,

When I saw your letter appear in the postman's hand, I nearly fainted with joy. I recognised your handwriting on the envelope immediately. How could I not, after all those secret notes we used to pass back and forth at all hours of the day and night.

You will never be a terrible anything. These past few months have been hard on us all. Jimmy was such a big part of our family that we all fell his loss keenly. You are starting to sound like me, in denial about having twins. Although, I think I knew deep down that I wasn't just having one baby. A mother knows these things. I remember feeling a foot or a movement every time I shifted in the bed or moved my arm. Don't even get me started on when I went to the lavatory.

I can feel the air changing, I think your due date is soon.

Write soon, I am sending the biggest hug down to London with this letter.

Elizabeth.

Monday, 16 April 1945

Jimmy,

Our child grows restless. He wants to come and meet everyone. But most of all, he wants to meet his brave and handsome father. I fear it is almost time and you still aren't here. I want to keep the baby safe in my womb forever until the day you finally come home to us.

Saturday, 21 April 1945

Dear Elizabeth,

Yesterday, I gave birth to a lovely baby boy. He has Jimmy's eyes. I have decided to call him Freddie James Fitz, so that he knows he shares the name of a great man who would go to the ends of the earth for him. I wish Jimmy were here to share in my joy. I looked at my son's face and felt a joy that I can't put into words. I have named Peggy godmother, a role which she has gladly accepted.

Every time I hear a noise downstairs or outside, I jump up, thinking it is Jimmy, but it never is. I am not giving up hope that Jimmy will return to me, to us and when he does, there will be another little face to greet him and welcome him home.

I have no clue if Jimmy received my letter telling him I was pregnant, or whether he was declared missing before that. Letters always seem to take a while to get to their correct address, especially on the front lines. When Jimmy comes home, he may be in for the shock of his life, seeing a miniature him lying in the pram. I'll come visit soon, Freddie will love meeting his cousins.

Daisy and Freddie.

Saturday, 21 April 1945

Dear Mother and Father,

Yesterday saw the birth of my lovely baby boy. Holding him was like nothing I have ever experienced. Looking into his eyes, I can see Jimmy reflected back at me.

I am going to call him Freddie James, so that he knows he has the name of one of the bravest men I know.

In a few weeks, we will make the trip down to Kent so that you can officially meet your newest grandson.

Love,

Daisy and Freddie.

Monday, 23 April 1945

Dear Daisy,

This letter is from all of us, Mother and Father included. The twins are as unimpressed as only small babies can be, but one day they will appreciate the news of a younger cousin to play with. Mother and Father are so happy. We all are. Mother is looking smug at correctly predicting when you were going to give birth. Not that we were gambling on the birth of your child.

Now all we need is the end of the war and the return of Jimmy, and we will be all out of good news.

Give Freddie a kiss from us all.

Elizabeth.

Wednesday, 25 April 1945

My darling Jimmy,

On the 20th of April, you became a father to a beautiful, brown-eyed boy with a tiny tuft of dark brown hair. He looks just like you. I've called your son, our son, Freddie James. He gives me hope for the future and hope for your speedy return.

Saturday, 28 April 1945

Dear Daisy,

I am overjoyed about another grandson. I bet you're glad he wasn't part of a set, like your sister got. I know you would have loved twins, but they are a handful. Especially when they are you and your sister, always making mischief.

Come down to Kent as soon as you can. I want to take Freddie, Vera, and Keith for a walk in the village, making sure to proudly show off my three grandchildren! All the other members of the WI have one grandchild, some with two (a few years apart, mind you) but I can show off my three!

That aside, it would be lovely for the both of you to come down to Kent soon. Your father and I look forward to meeting our newest grandson. Much love to you both.
Mother.

Tuesday, 1 May 1945

Dear Elizabeth,

Freddie is being wonderful. He is growing so fast. At this rate, Jimmy is going to come home to see a fully grown adult instead of the tiny baby he is now. I have had him christened, just a quick service at our local church. Only Peggy, Henry and I attended. And obviously Freddie. I know mother will be upset, but I am planning a big party in Kent for when Jimmy returns home. I just didn't want to leave to too late, not knowing when Jimmy will be coming back.

Peggy's mother came to visit and saw her holding Freddie. She assumed it was Peggy's baby and started cooing immediately. Peggy set her straight and honestly, she glared at me so hard, I felt chills. Peggy's mother didn't even take into consideration that she saw Peggy a few months ago looking decidedly not pregnant. It's like the woman substituted her braincells for wealth.

I cannot wait to get back into work. I just miss the children so much. I'll be taking a few months off though, to spend time with Freddie. The headmaster is giving me until September, which by then Jimmy may hopefully be home.

Much love to you all,

Daisy.

Friday, 4 May 1945

Dear Daisy,

I never want to meet Peggy's mother. She sounds like the worst possible person. Don't let her near Freddie too much, we don't want her corrupting him.

I understand why you had a quick christening. Mother not so much. I have compromised with her, and she is now planning a huge party with the whole village in mandatory attendance. I fear it will be a bigger celebration than the king's coronation!

Harry and Henry are causing mischief, and Mother is getting quite cross with them. She has threatened to send them over to me if they keep misbehaving. I don't know what she expects me to do, I'm the one who has been encouraging their not-so-pleasant behaviour. I have no doubt that mother will get her revenge when the twins are old enough to start terrorising Billy and me.

Don't rush back to work. I know you miss it, but nothing beats the first few months of your baby's life, watching them grow and change before your very eyes.

Hugs and kisses,
Elizabeth.

The London Gazette *8 May 1945*

VE-DAY FINALLY HERE!

Troops stop fighting as Hitler surrenders war to allied troops.

On this momentous day, troops across Europe ceased fire! The last shell was fired, and the last troop's gun was lifted. Soldiers will start returning, and while we celebrate their return, we also hold a place in our hearts for the fallen. The king will be making a speech and a toast to commemorate the fallen in the next few days. While victory reins amongst troops and their families, we pray for those we lost, and for those whose lives have been horribly affected during this bleak period of our lives.

Wednesday, 9 May 1945

Dear Elizabeth,

Have you heard the news? If you haven't, then you must have been living under a rock. The Germans have surrendered! We have won! And you know what that means, Jimmy can finally come home. Even after all these months, I haven't given up hope. Freddie is too young to understand what is happening, that he is part of a momentous part of history.

To celebrate, we are having a street party, everyone is going to bring as much food as our rations will allow. That's another thing, maybe now we can finally come off rations.

I cried so much upon reading the paper that I woke Freddie up from his nap. I couldn't believe it! Finally, this horrible war has ended, and life can go back to normal and my husband can finally come home.

Hugs and smiles all round. I don't think there isn't a person in England not celebrating this.

Love,

Daisy.

Saturday, 12 May 1945

Dear Daisy,

Yes! The war is over! Maybe rationing will finally end, and I won't have to keep saving up my ration coupons for special occasions. The end of the war does mean the return of soldiers though, just protect your heart. Jimmy may yet still come home but I doubt it will be immediately. And you may have to face the fact that he may never come home.

I feel absolutely horrible for saying all this, but I am your sister, your twin, and if anyone was going to get through to you, then it would be me.

I keep praying every night, that Jimmy will return, and I won't stop until he is. I just don't want you to live the rest of your life thinking he might come home.

The twins have started rolling and trying to ease themselves up to crawl. I don't know what I'll do when they start walking. I'll have to hide all the breakable objects!

We all love you so much and are here for you no matter what happens.

Elizabeth.

Tuesday, 15 May 1945

Dear Elizabeth,

I have been holding onto hope since I received the letter about Jimmy. In the beginning, I didn't want to believe what was written in black and white in front of me. I didn't want to believe that my soulmate had been taken from me. So many people across the country will have loved ones not returning home, and I couldn't bring myself to admit that I might be joining them. Over the months, feeling Freddie grow inside me, feeling his kicking, hearing his heartbeat, has given me strength.

I know that Jimmy may never return home, may never see his son, but there is a tiny sliver of my heart that still hopes I will see him again.

If I give up now, what will I have to live for? I could never remarry. Jimmy is my kindred soul, the only one for me, my one true love.

Thank you though, for always looking out for me. Where would I be without you supporting my good decisions and egging on my bad ones?

When Vera and Keith start walking, lock the doors! I fully suspect that they will be completely like us. Like Harry and Henry are now.

Much love,

Daisy.

Friday, 18 May 1945

Dearest Jimmy,

Freddie grows bigger every day. Now that the war is over, I pray for your speedy return. I know in my heart of hearts that you're still alive and that somehow you will come back to us, back to me.

Our son needs his father, needs his strong arms to hold him close and make the world right again.

Come home, Jimmy …

Saturday, 19 May 1945

Dear Daisy,

We are all living with hope for Jimmy, for you all to be reunited again.

I have some slightly joyous news. I am pregnant, again. Three months by the nurse's count. I sat in the clinic in shock. I didn't even think you could get pregnant this soon after giving birth. I went home and told Billy. You probably heard his jaw dropping and hitting the floor all the way in London. Nevertheless, we are both ecstatic. I've always said that I wanted as many children as I could manage. And the new baby will be close in age to the twins.

I didn't think I would have to go through the whole pregnancy thing quite so soon. Can you imagine? I'll have to go on bed rest again! At least this time, there will be no war on.

Love to both you and Freddie,

Elizabeth.

Monday, 21 May 1945

Dear Daisy,

How are you doing? How is my gorgeous grandson? The war is finally, over so now I might be able to ask the agricultural officer if I can finally have my flower beds back. I grew prize winning flowers before the war, you know.

I know you must be missing the children at the school terribly. Elizabeth mentioned that you aren't returning until September, which I think is very sensible. Back in my day, mothers stayed at home regardless but then I suppose that is the effects of the war for you.

Speaking of your sister, did you hear, she is pregnant again? Your father actually laughed solidly for about ten minutes upon hearing the news. Come and visit soon.

Love,

Mother.

Wednesday, 23 May 1945

Dear Elizabeth,

I can't believe you are pregnant again! And so soon! It seems like yesterday I received your letter with news of the twins. Not that we knew they were twins back then. At least this time, you will have the twins to keep you entertained.

I went into school yesterday to see the headmaster. It is apparently a normal meeting. He just wanted to check in, see how I was doing after having the baby. I had to take Freddie in with me. All my neighbours work and besides, I can't bear to be separated from him just yet. The headmaster gave him a good cuddle and bounced him on his knee.

I also went and visited my class; some children recognised me, and some were new, but all welcomed me with open arms. The vicar is taking my class until I come back in September, something which the children are less than thrilled about. I reassured them that I would be back before they could blink.

Give my love to everyone.

Daisy.

Saturday, 26 May 1945

Dear Mother,

I'm going back into school after the summer holidays. I need to go back, not just for the money, but I miss all the children. They filled a hole after finding out Jimmy was missing in action. They made the days bearable.

The weather is becoming absolutely lovely. I am currently writing this letter at the park. Freddie is napping in the pram, and I have hitched my skirt up slightly, letting the golden rays soak into my skin.

Now that the war is over, when will Harry and Henry go back to London? I popped into school the other day to meet with the headmaster and saw quite a few children had returned.

Please for the love of God stop going on about your 'prize winning' flowerbeds. You still need to be growing vegetables; we are still on rations, you know.

Love to you all,

Daisy.

Tuesday, 29 May 1945

Dear Daisy,

I told the girls at work that I was pregnant again, mostly happy, but a few cross because they said, and I quote here 'I was the best manager they have and couldn't imagine working under anyone else'. I'm not even kidding, they actually said that. No bribes necessary.

I saw your comment about mother's flower beds. I can't believe you actually said it. We've been thinking that for years! I thought mother was going to bury us alive when we ran through them one spring. And then trampled soil and petals through into the living room.

Do you know when you are coming down to Kent? We all miss you terribly and long to meet baby Freddie. And soon, I'll be incapable of moving past the front door, so you had better come and visit.

Write soon,

Elizabeth.

Friday, 1 June 1945

Dear Daisy,

We heard from Harry and Henry's parents. They are coming to pick them up on Wednesday. I will be sad to see them go. We all will. They have been such a joy to look after. I think your father will miss them the most, not just for their free labour, but for the company in the fields and having people to actually laugh at his jokes.

I've invited them for dinner, so we can all meet each other, which I am looking forward to. I've told your father to make sure he wears his good socks. Give Freddie a big kiss from me.

Mother.

Wednesday, 6 June 1945

Dear Elizabeth,

I heard about Harry and Henry going back to London. Mother is quite upset, although she has conveniently forgotten about all the trauma they have put her and father through. If she misses the mischief, she can soon train the twins to start causing riots. But at least Keith and Vera aren't identical, so rules out most of the pranks we used to pull as children.

I think father might actually start crying when Harry and Henry go. He won't admit it, but he is so fond of those boys.

I will be coming down to Kent in a few weeks. Not for the big christening party mother is planning, but for you all to meet Freddie. And I haven't seen you all in so long. I feel like years has passed since last time I saw you.

I'll write to confirm my train times. Maybe you could meet me at the station with the twins.

Love,
Daisy and Freddie.

Saturday, 9 June 1945

Dear Mr and Mrs Franklin, Elizabeth, and Billy,

Yesterday, Daisy, the baby and I all went for a nice walk, soaking up the brilliant summer sunshine. Upon arriving back home, we stood outside, having a chat and sharing a cigarette when we saw a silhouette of a person walking down the road. As the figure came closer, we could make out the hunched and shadowed features of a soldier, returning home from overseas. Daisy – and I must admit, me – had been getting our hopes up, seeing soldiers returning home every day, only to have them dashed again when none of these poor men turned out to be Jimmy.

But this figure drew closer. We both gasped in surprise. Jimmy was finally home! Leaving the pram with me, Daisy ran the rest of the way down the street and into his waiting arms. He looks drawn and tired and somehow older, but no visible injuries, and I am sure that you will receive a long and lengthy letter from Daisy in the coming days.

Together, the reunited couple walked back to where I was standing. I reached out and hugged Jimmy for myself and welcomed him home.

Pulling apart, he then noticed the baby and looked at me, but I shook my head. Daisy picked up the baby and held him out to his father.

'Jimmy', she said, 'I think it's time you met your son, Freddie James Fitz'.

At this, Jimmy just stood there and wept. He picked his son out of Daisy's arms and cradled him close, kissing his brow and whispering to him. Before seeing the baby, his face had looked aged and his shoulders crumpled, but this tiny human filled him with so much joy and love that it shone out of his face, brightening the world.

The four of us returned upstairs where we said our goodbyes. I offered to take baby Freddie for the night, but Daisy shook her head with a smile. I think that they just wanted some time as a new family, just the three of them.

Much love,

Peggy.